While We Dream

A Collection of Fiction

by Mark Le Dain

Dedication

To Meredith

Contents

Environment

Nelson walked downstairs as the early morning sun filtered through the windows. His feet were familiar with each step, and he didn't turn on any lights to avoid waking the family. It was his favorite time of day, and no one else would be up for hours. He made a cup of tea and went to the living room to read. He opened the window and let cold mountain air filter in. That was when he heard the low rumble of the garage opening. Running to the garage door he opened it just in time to see Madison pulling in. She wasn't in the government issued all-terrain vehicle though; she was in his vintage diesel BMW.

"Oh my god, Madison, what are you doing?"

"Daddy, I was careful, not a scratch. See, you can trust me."

His voice was shaky. "How long were you driving?"

"It was just a small party and then I stayed over. No big deal. My friends said you have the coolest taste in cars."

"How much fuel?"

Madison was quiet as she realized what her dad was asking. "I... I don't know."

Nelson leaned in and looked at the fuel gauge. It was almost at zero.

He ran back into the house at a sprint.

"Dad?!"

Nelson took the stairs two at a time and ran into his bedroom. "Mary! Wake up. Turn everything off, everything. Madison drove the BMW all night. Cut power remotely to the cottage, I don't care if it freezes." Mary slowly woke, and then, realizing the gravity of the situation, jumped on her tablet and made a call. Nelson had already run back out of the room and was now shouting at the kids to wake up.

"Felix! Paige! I need you to get up and power everything down right now. If you have any products you ordered that haven't been made yet, cancel the order. Same with clothes. Paige, power down any atmosphere controls you have at your college dorm."

"Dad! All my plants will die."

"I don't care. I think we went over."

Nelson ran through a final check of the house to make sure everything was off. When he returned, his family had silently collected in the kitchen. They all understood what had happened. There was no sound except for the intermittent sniffle out of Madison.

"I'm sorry. I forgot we took those flights this month. I..." Madison's lips were shaky as she spoke.

Nelson pulled her in. "It's okay. We are together and okay. That's all that matters." His breathing was returning as time passed, and his thoughts got more hopeful. It had already been ten minutes; maybe they were going to be okay. It would be difficult for the rest of the month but there were only three days left. He knew they could do it. They couldn't eat meat but there were enough vegetables in the garden. He could go without food if he needed to. He was thinking through the solutions when he heard the sirens in the distance.

"That could be anything," Mary whispered.

No one spoke or moved as the siren grew louder. Nelson knew. He broke from the group and put one foot ahead of the other as he slowly walked down the hallway to the front door. He was almost at the door when the knock came. With one hand on the doorknob, Nelson turned and looked at his family. "I love all of you so much. And I know you feel the same."

He opened the door to see the bright blue of the police uniform. The officer stepped forward and began to read from his tablet.

"Your residence has exceeded the carbon threshold required to live in this jurisdiction. By orders of the President, we have the right to halt all carbon impact activity, including those related to food and drink. If you need either, you will be provided with a government issued intravenous solution until your new carbon credits are issued. Within five days you are required to relocate to the carbon output jurisdiction that meets your new threshold. We will have ascertained what that level is shortly. Are there any questions before we commence preparations for the assisted relocation program?"

Nelson looked at the officer and back at his family. "It was me alone. I was the reason the threshold was exceeded. I took a joyride in an old diesel car. You will find it registered to me."

The policeman had his head down, scrolling through his tablet for the requisite paperwork, but he lifted it up and smiled at the news that he now only had one form to complete. “That is perfectly within your rights, sir. It will be only you that is processed then, assuming the family will not be joining you.”

Nelson turned to see Mary clutching Felix and Paige a few steps back. They had their faces pressed against her. Madison stood alone to the side, with tears pouring down her face. It looked as if she was going to open her mouth, but Nelson gave all of them a shake of his head.

“Okay, then,” the officer seemed to be in a hurry. I will be back in a few days, and all the relevant details are in your email. You just need to take a photo for identification.” The officer pulled up his tablet, snapped the photo, nodded, and then closed the door behind him. The family stood in the foyer, staring at the closed door, and no one could find the words.

—— «» ——

Nelson dropped his bags on the ground and collapsed on the bed. It had been two weeks of travel. He looked around the tiny apartment. It felt as if dust or soot had touched everything. He walked to the window and opened the blinds slowly to see the dark red sky. The city stretched for miles ahead of him, and he could see another superstorm forming in the distance. He hadn't been planning on opening the window but suddenly realized it wasn't even an option with the way the building was designed. He shook as he spoke the word. “Earth.”

While We Dream

I opened my eyes and threw up. The smell of vomit balanced out the antiseptic smell of the goo surrounding me. It was hard to believe a year had passed.

"Roy, that stinks," Dave said. "Just my luck. My pod is next to yours, not some beautiful girl's."

I looked at Dave. His pod had released him moments before mine. Color was returning to his face.

"Let's be honest, Dave, if a beautiful girl were in this pod, you would have broken her heart thirty years ago."

Dave grinned. "You know me, kid. They say the world is overpopulated, but we could always use a few more women. They still seem tough for me to find." He had a coughing fit as he got his bearings. He was probably fifty, which was old these days. People weren't living long due to the sleep cycles; it was too much strain on the body.

"You have a job you need to get to?" Dave asked.

"You ask me every year, and every year, I explain that I synthesize vanadium for these pods of ours."

"See, that's why every year I forget. Sounds boring as hell."

The announcements interrupted our laughter: "*Welcome to the start of your cycle. Please collect your possessions before the switch takes place. Your previous habitats await.*"

Dave and I quickly shook hands and headed for different exits.

The cycles were created when Earth was unable to support more people. Other suitable habitats had not been found. I wasn't alive during the pre-cycle days, but we were taught about it in school. It got so bad near the end that governments were debating culls before the solution of the cycles was finally proposed. It was the type of solution a child would suggest; you tell them there are too many people, and they say, "Why don't half sleep while the other half are awake?" The idea worked. You went into suspended animation for a year, and it became someone else's turn to live their year. Suddenly, Earth had five billion people at once instead of ten. The key was staggering the start times of the sleep year worldwide. This was obvious, as essential services needed to keep running when populations switched. And you couldn't skip between zones to dodge your sleep cycle. It was a civic duty to sleep, like the drafts in the global wars of the twenty-first century. Dodgers were strictly punished.

I gathered my possessions and headed to my habitat, a white cube with square windows. People became less interested in their homes when they realized someone else would live there half the time. The rich could afford to rent their houses to themselves while they slept, but that luxury was not available to me. I put my clothes away and took a real nap. The next day I started my job for the seventeenth time since leaving school.

A week later, an explosion devastated an adjacent zone's largest vanadium mine. The organization I worked for was in charge of the vanadium supply for four of the world's ten zones. It was an important job; the last thing you wanted was someone's pod battery dying. They asked me firmly to assist the zone where the explosion took place. With the mine's production halted, more vanadium synthesizers were required to compensate for the shortfall. I was shocked by the request, as people were rarely permitted to leave their zone. I was still crafting my protest when I found myself on a helicopter headed north.

It was that day that I met Naomi. When I arrived, she greeted me on the platform. Naomi was tall and slender, dressed in a lab coat with a yellow leaf embroidered on the back. "Do you want to get your head chopped off? Why are you here?" she shouted. She had seemed very pleasant before opening the helicopter doors.

"I'm Roy. I'm here to help." She was unsatisfied, so I added, "I wasn't happy with this either, even less so after that reception."

She smirked and said, "Follow me."

She cheered up after we got inside. "I'm sorry about earlier. You seemed too handsome to have brains, so I figured they were sending management to take over my operation."

"No problem. You can't be too smart yourself, though, if your attractiveness indicator has any truth to it." She laughed, a beautiful floating laugh.

—— «» ——

Naomi and I lay in bed five months later. "Roy, we need to talk about this. I go off-cycle in a month." It was a fact I hadn't been able to face, and I lay there silently.

"I can't bear the thought of not spending half my life with you," I finally said. "I honestly don't know what to do."

"I have one idea, but it's crazy," she said.

I moved closer to her and whispered in her ear, "Is it to murder me so we can be together forever and ever?" She laughed and shoved me.

"I'm serious, Roy. What if I hide next cycle? I go into hiding, and you head back. You will be asleep in your pod while I make my way south. I have some contacts at the transport office. It will be a good story to tell our kids about how their lazy father slept while their mother made the journey."

"No, it's too risky. What if we get separated? I found you once by chance. I don't want to count on finding you again."

"We can't hide like fugitives. What would that give us? A few years? I'm talking about being apart only so we can be together forever."

"I know what you're saying." I was frustrated and slammed my hand against the pillow. It startled her.

"Are you really that angry?"

"No. I'm not angry. I'm scared. You don't understand. I'm the one that will need to find you. What if I can't? I won't even get to tell you how bad your idea was."

She giggled, but she could see how upset I was. "We don't have to decide right now. We have time."

I nodded, but deep down, I knew this was the only way.

One month later, I squeezed Naomi. "I love you. Leave me a note in the dirt in front of my habitat. Tell me where to find you, and we'll start a real life together." I held her close. The decision to leave her tore at me.

She broke our embrace. "You need to go. It's okay."

"It feels wrong leaving you. I only just found you."

"You're only leaving so that we can spend forever together. Remember that. It will feel like no time has passed when you wake up. No time at all."

I nodded, wiped my eyes, and headed to my zone.

For the next six months, I was a zombie. I waited to sleep only so I could wake up and see Naomi. As I finally stepped back into my pod, I thought of our future together. I closed my eyes.

—— «» ——

I awoke. I did not puke. I said a distracted hello to Dave and sprinted to the habitat. The ground was covered in the dust of our world. I dug on my hands and knees until I found what I knew was there. A small tin box with a yellow leaf on the front. When I opened it, dozens of handwritten notes spilled out. I smiled. I wouldn't have been able to write Naomi only one note, either. I looked for the first one.

I love you. I'm at 6507 on Elk Street. I'm already planning our first meal.

The following note was different. It was crumpled.

Roy, I don't understand why you didn't come yesterday. I don't know what's happening. Please come back to me.

I was shocked and furiously flipped to the next.

I looked you up to see if you had died during sleep. I hoped you had. I could understand that better than you leaving me. There's no record of your death. No one is giving me any answers. I'm sorry for wanting it, I hate that you left me alone.

The last note had utterly different handwriting, shaky and frail. It was barely recognizable as Naomi's.

Roy, part of me still misses you. Thirty years on, I let go of the hate, but the love remains. I've lived as a fugitive since changing zones. I never went back on-cycle. There has been some beauty in my life, but it has been challenging. In my final days now, I often think of you. I hope you found happiness.

I read them all. My mouth was dry. I was motionless, with my knees in the dirt, as tears rolled down my face. I now understood what Naomi hadn't. I had always felt we were producing too much power for just five billion people. Part of me had once thought there might be a third or fourth cycle, kept secret to avoid panic. I had no idea when the last note had been written, but I now knew for sure there were well over 100 billion people, sleeping and awake, on this planet. And none of them was the one I wanted.

Friends of the Family

Angela was confused as she watched her dad talking to himself on the television. Not only did she not understand how he was in two places, but she also didn't understand the words he was using. They were shouting about something, and then her father stopped talking and stormed upstairs. She looked at the image of her dad on the television that now had no one to speak with. They briefly made eye contact and then he looked away. She opened her mouth to speak but the television went black.

"Mommy, that man Daddy was talking to on the television..." She had trouble forming the question. "Does Daddy have a brother?"

Denise hated this conversation. Over the past few weeks, Angela has been asking her mother the same question in one form or another. Parenting literature says to be honest with your children, but Denise felt children should never have to think about certain things. The moment they did, they were no longer children.

"That man is a copy of Daddy that helps Daddy with his work. You know how Cynthia helps with our chores around the house?"

Angela nodded as she put her spoon in her mouth.

"Well, this is the same, except instead of being a different person, like Cynthia, he looks just like Daddy. This way, he can do the same work Daddy does."

Angela nodded. Denise prayed that Angela was satisfied with the answers but worried she might simply be chewing. The seconds passed, and Denise thought she was safe. She started cleaning the breakfast dishes.

"Why doesn't Cynthia look like you?"

Denise had almost made it to the sink with the dishes. There were two honest answers she could give. The first was that Denise had picked Cynthia for the very fact that she looked so distinctly different, with her broad shoulders and long chin, because if she had picked someone resembling anything close to a traditional woman, Daddy would have tried to have sex with her. The second possible answer concerns economics. Denise decided to go with the second answer.

"Getting someone made exactly like you costs a lot of money. Because of the cost, you only do it for important jobs like your dad's, which only certain people can do. This means more people can be out there saving lives like Daddy. Does that make sense?"

"Sure. Thanks, Mommy."

Angela lowered herself from her seat at the ten-person kitchen table. She had lost interest in the conversation and ran upstairs. The sunlight and sea breeze filtered in through the doors to the yard. Denise put the rest of the dishes in the sink for Cynthia to take care of and then headed upstairs to prepare for the day.

Mike was in the master bathroom, so she decided to go down the hall. There was a time in their relationship when they would have gotten ready together, but that was many years ago. A sense of privacy, secrecy, or possibly even dislike had crept into their lives. When she got back, he was still getting ready. He must have taken another call, which delayed him.

"I'm going to drive Angela to school and then do yoga. I'll be back around noon, and Cynthia will be here. Good luck in surgery."

There was no reply. She rested her hand on the doorknob to check on him, but he finally responded.

"Sounds good."

She and her husband had now completed their beautiful exchange for the day. She headed downstairs and took Angela to school.

Denise pulled back into their cul-de-sac. The house looked different as she drove up. At first, she couldn't understand what looked so out of place until she realized Mike's car was still in the driveway. The fact it shocked her showed how little he was home. It was a dark blue electric convertible. Mike was always torn between parking the car in the garage for security and parking it outside to show the neighbors. He was torn in the sense that he always parked it outside but hated the risk.

As Denise pulled in, she gave the car a wide berth. She had never scratched it, yet Mike perpetually scolded her to be careful. Sometimes, she wanted to hit it; if he was already angry, she might as well have done it. As she opened the garage door, smoke started billowing out. A coughing fit consumed her, and she had to close her watering eyes. When she opened them, the air had cleared, and she could see the source of the smoke; Mike's antique Ford Mustang sat there running. The entirety of the scene had yet to register with Denise; her first thought was how annoyed she was with the mess. Finally, her mind comprehended the motionless body in the driver's seat. Out of context, she wouldn't have recognized him as Mike. There was a color to him that was more like a fish than a man. She screamed and ran to him.

"Mike!"

She threw open the car door and shook him, but there was no response. He had no pulse, and his color and temperature confirmed he had been gone for some time. A weird smirk crossed her face as she thought about how this doctor thing was easy.

He clutched a tablet in his hand. The only item on the screen was a note. Denise picked it up and read.

> *Mr. Canon, our apologies for the delayed reply. We wanted to review your case in full. As a result of our careful diligence, we have decided that you alone are responsible for the malpractice suit brought against your clone and, by association, yourself in Maryland. It's always been the practice that the owner of clones is required to purchase additional personal insurance if those clones perform any task that could result in personal liability risk. Based on historical records and your extensive personal experience with clones, it appears you were fully aware of this risk and chose to avoid the insurance and the associated fees in their entirety. Failure to purchase insurance was equivalent to breaching your employment contract with the hospital, and therefore, they have no obligation to protect you further in this lawsuit. We advise you to pay the thirteen million in damages and waste no more of our time, the hospitals, or your time. You're being allowed to keep your license and your other clones only because of your historical contributions to medicine. Many of these contributions occurred before you had any of your existing wealth; maybe this financial setback will cause you to start genuinely contributing again. I hope you know that I continue to remain a friend, but the views contained in this letter are shared by the other board members and me.*
>
> *Sincerely,*
>
> *Martin Rytz, Chairman, Global Health Services Council*

Any sadness Denise had felt quickly became anger. She kicked the car.

"You coward! How could you leave with all of this? How could you leave us? You've ruined us, and you're too pathetic even to help clean things up. You have a daughter! Your damn pride..."

She smashed her hand against the side of the car again and again until she finally slumped down beside it out of exhaustion. Denise knew they were already dangerously close to being broke before this lawsuit. Mike had taken out several loans to make all the clones. There were eight in total now, and they were not cheap. He'd promised her that the clones would make it all back in no time and then some. With a shock that rivaled seeing her dead husband, she realized that all his clones would now be decommissioned. Clones weren't permitted to exist without their human counterpart. They were viewed exclusively as an extension of an individual; the rules were as much for people's sanity as anything else.

In a daze, Denise started walking into the house. She had to call the police, and she had to get in touch with Angela. They'd need to sell the house, and she'd have to find Mike's insurance policy. She suddenly wondered if the suicide had voided it. Perhaps she could make it look like an accident. Her mind was spinning with everything that needed to be done. Four minutes later, she realized she was still standing in the middle of the house; she hadn't moved.

"Hello?"

She was so startled that she screamed. Denise turned around to see Mike's clone on the kitchen screen. The one from Boston. It was impossibly weird for her to see him alive when she now knew exactly what he looked like dead.

"Sorry, I didn't mean to startle you, ma'am. Mike around? I wanted to chat with him about who will attend the upcoming round of medical conferences in Europe?" He chatted away as if it was any regular day. And to him, it was; he was not aware that he lay dead only a few meters from where she stood.

The only words she could get out were, "He's busy."

"No problem. I'll connect with him another time. Have a good day."

"Wait! Sorry, I've had a lot on the go and was flustered. I almost forgot to give you a message from him. He needs you to come to the house... to our home here, this afternoon."

"Can you get him to come tell me that, please?"

“As I said, he’s busy. But he needs you to come to the house. I don’t see why you need him to convey that message. I can assure you he would deliver the message in a much less attractive way.” She wondered if this Mike was not yet sick of her flirting.

“I’m sorry, ma’am, but I need to hear from him. I can only act as a representative for him. If I take direction from others, then there’s no consistency. I must be certain I’m acting as he would act.”

Denise thought that if his goal was to act like Mike, then he was doing a great job by ignoring her and making things difficult.

“You’re telling me that if you don’t hear from Mike, you’re simply going to work all day and then stay home all night?”

Mike scoffed. “Yes, exactly. A day is a day. No need to say it in such an argumentative fashion. Hey, I must go. There’s a lot to do today.” The screen went black.

Denise ran upstairs and packed a bag. She suddenly remembered Cynthia would be arriving soon and called her.

“I need you to pick Angela up from school and take her to your place for a few days.”

“Okay. I can do that. What should I tell her?”

“Thank you. Tell her Mommy and Daddy had to go away for work. We’re sorry, but we’ll be back very soon, and she should stay with you until then. I’ll let you know when she can return.”

This wasn’t the first time that Cynthia had needed to take Angela for a few days; usually, it was related to Mike’s temper, and sometimes even Denise's. There was never violence, but if they were arguing, Denise didn’t want Angela to see that. They stopped blaming these arguments on passion many years ago. Denise thought that the one good thing that came out of those arguments was that Cynthia had no questions about the arrangement.

Denise walked back into the garage and passed Mike’s body.

“Goodbye, dear. I’m taking the convertible for a spin.” She smiled and quickly closed the garage door behind her. Denise wasn’t running. A plan was forming in her head, and she was headed to Boston.

Denise pulled up outside Mike's condo in Boston. It felt weird thinking of him as "Mike" but that was who he was. That was who each of them was. She turned her headlights off and watched him from her car. He had turned on his condo lights in response to the darkening sky. Watching him was mesmerizing. She had always wondered how the clones lived. Denise pictured them going into a bag or cylinder each night; it was an antiquated image that had grown out of her childhood love for science fiction. Instead of something bizarre, she watched him eat dinner in front of the TV. The same scene was mimicked in his neighbor's condo and the one three doors down. The apartment was exceptionally modest. A low-rise two-bedroom condo in an average part of town. As she thought about it, perhaps it was only modest compared to her husband's taste. The contrast could be easily explained; her husband received ninety percent of a clone's wages for bringing them into this world. She wondered why Mike wasn't sitting at his table studying. If he fell too far behind in knowledge, it was easier for Mike to clone his increasing knowledge than to teach the clone something new. Maybe he didn't understand this, or maybe he knew and didn't care. Or maybe it was no different than how she drank and smoked despite what she knew about consequences; perhaps he was exceptionally human. She was going to find out. Denise exited the car and walked up to the door of the condo.

The door was matte black. She made sure to stay on the left edge, against the wall, so that she wouldn't show up on camera; Denise didn't want him to see who it was. She rang the bell and waited. They needed to have their conversation inside. He opened the door, and a look of surprise registered on his face.

"What're you doing here?"

Before this, she'd had minimal interaction with the clones.

"My husband and I were in town, and he needed to speak with you. He just had to take a private call around the corner. I'm not important enough to be allowed to hear what he's talking about." She rolled her eyes for effect. "Can I wait inside? It's cold out."

He hesitated but then smiled, narcissistically, at Denise not being allowed to listen to Mike's call. Denise had known that would get him to let his guard down. He opened the door wider and gestured for her to enter. She crossed the threshold and closed the door behind her.

"Can we sit down while we wait?" She pointed at the couch. "Please."

He nodded. As soon as they were both sitting, it was time.

"Mike is dead. He died this morning. I need your help."

The words didn't register with him, so she repeated, "Mike is dead."

"I need to talk to Mike." There was confusion in his eyes. He was a bee without a queen. She put her hands on his shoulders.

"You can't talk to him. He's dead!"

"Why are you telling me this instead of the police?"

"Because we can't let them find out. You need to understand that as soon as they find out—"

"No!" He cut her off. "You're trying to trick me. I could tell that something was wrong this morning on the video chat. Mike doesn't want any of this. I need to call the authorities."

He got up and started to walk to his phone on the counter. He was going to unravel everything she had built. Denise thought of her daughter. She didn't care about the house or the cars; those were things that Mike had built. She cared only about the life of her daughter. That was what she had built, and now Mike would destroy it. With anger building inside her, she grabbed Mike's arm.

"You can't! You're a self-interested moron, but you aren't working in your own self-interest right now. This isn't helping you. They will get rid of you!"

He turned and threw her on the floor.

"I save lives. No one's getting rid of me. I contribute to the world. What do you do?"

He left her on the floor and went to pick up his phone. For all Mike's bravado and strength, she knew his neck was exceptionally sensitive. On vacation, he caught a tennis ball in his Adam's apple, which took him the entire trip to recover. She stood up and called out to him one more time.

"Mike!"

He turned, and she punched him as hard as she could in the neck. He dropped the phone and keeled over, gasping for air. His face looked like it might explode if it couldn't find an outlet for his anger. Unable to speak, he writhed in agony on the floor. He slowly put a hand on his knee and steadied himself to rise. She casually picked up the lamp from the table nearby and brought it down on his head with a thud. It was heavy, with a beautiful marble bottom, some of Mike's taste shining through.

Remembering how visible the condo had been from the parking lot, she quickly ran to the window. No one appeared to be out there. She drew the curtains. Picking up his phone, she read through all the messages. It looked as if he was not expecting any company tonight. There was no time to waste. She exited the apartment, closed the door, and headed to her car.

As she pulled out of the parking lot, she had to smile to herself. A day ago, she had been fighting with her husband over the renovations at their cottage, and today, she had two of him dead in the eastern United States. She sang along to the music in the car and turned onto the highway. She needed to go to Baltimore.

It was exceptionally late when she arrived in Baltimore. She couldn't remember if the Baltimore clone had been cleared to practice surgery again or if he would be at his apartment. Denise headed to his apartment, hoping he wouldn't be away on the night shift. He'd be groggy if he were at home, but that didn't strike her as a bad thing. The clone lived in a brick loft in an old heritage building. She didn't want to warn him by buzzing up, so she snuck in behind a young, drunk couple and followed them into the building.

She rang the door, but there was no answer. She rang again. It opened a crack, and there stood Mike. He was in his boxers and wiping the sleep from his eyes.

"I'm Mike's wife. I desperately need to talk to you."

He looked at her with rare sympathy. "Uh, okay, please come in."

Denise followed him into the apartment. It was messier than what she'd expected. It looked like it belonged to a man who'd recently undergone a nasty breakup.

He turned and looked at her. "Sorry for the state of things. I wasn't expecting anyone. Let me put some clothes on."

He had a strength to him that Mike had lost many years back; it was the very same definition that had attracted her to Mike. She watched him walk away. He returned from his room wearing an oversized shirt and sweats.

"Would you like some tea?" he asked. "I'm making some."

"That'd be lovely."

He got two cups and brought them over. Compared to the others, he was disarming. Denise wondered if it was self-doubt she was seeing. Mike poured the tea, and the two sat across from each other in silence. The night carried on outside the large windows of the loft.

Denise broke the silence. "What happened in surgery? The one you're being sued for."

Mike sighed and put his head in his hands. It was a position her husband would have avoided; there was a vulnerability to it that he would have found unbecoming. His voice was shaky when he spoke.

"My patient woke up during surgery. The anesthesia hadn't been properly administered. I was nearing the end of the procedure when I heard her scream. I couldn't finish the procedure. I couldn't focus on anything but her screams. The other doctors refused to administer additional anesthesia in case an adverse reaction was what caused her to wake up. They asked me to finish quickly. She kept screaming. All I had to do was keep going, the machines do most of it anyway, but I froze. I couldn't believe that I was causing someone that much pain. By the time another doctor stepped in, it was too late. She bled out."

He paused and took a sip of his tea.

"There was a serenity to surgery before that day. The patient was silent, and all I knew about them was that they would be better once I was done. That was my world. I had done medical school and other things before ... but that seemed like another lifetime. I suppose it was; it was your husband's lifetime. Once I saw more, I wasn't entirely sure where I fit. Six years in this life, and yet it suddenly felt so uncertain. I suppose I've been trying to find my purpose since."

Denise walked over to him and put his head against her chest. She smelled the top of his head. Denise hadn't held Mike like this since his breakdown during medical school. It sounded as if he was starting to cry.

"Are you here to decommission me?"

She looked down at him and softly whispered, "No, I'm here to save you."

Mike looked up at her. Their faces were impossibly close. Denise did something she hadn't come to do. She kissed him. He tasted of sweat and alcohol. Her fingers ran their way through his hair at a quickening pace. This was

Mike. This wasn't Mike. She didn't know or care; she only knew she wanted a part of him. He picked her up, his arms firm and strong, and placed her gently on the kitchen counter, his lips never leaving hers. He knew nothing about their arguments or betrayals. He'd never tasted her skin, never smelled her hair. She rubbed her face against his chest and gave in.

The two of them lay on the floor of the kitchen, naked in the moonlight. Denise's head rested on Mike's chest. She opened her eyes and, without any introduction, said, "Mike's dead."

He sat up. "What do you mean?"

"My husband Mike is dead. As soon as the authorities realize he's dead, all of you will be decommissioned. You're legally an extension of his life and nothing more. That's why I came here tonight. I need your help."

"Are you certain he's dead?"

"Yes. I'm certain."

He seemed to accept this quickly. It probably came easier given Mike's agenda of having him decommissioned.

"Why do we have to be terminated when the original dies?"

Denise thought about how different the world had been when her daughter had asked similar questions. "When a person dies, their clones are destroyed. It prevents the concentration of wealth. If my husband had the most competitive genetics, and our family could simply clone more of him until the end of time, then our family would take a lot of wealth and jobs from everyone else. That's the reason they give. In reality, I think people are scared. We're trying to reintegrate a sense of mortality into what we've created. People can't handle the idea that you could exist separately from your original. If you can simply exist, it scares a lot of people. It forces us to ask ourselves: what have we created? It forces us to ask ourselves: what did God let us create?"

Denise looked Mike in the eyes. "I need your help because if they realize Mike is dead, they will decommission all our clones. I mean... you. We're so in debt that we'd be left with nothing. My daughter won't have the future I promised her, the future she deserves. Our daughter."

"What do you need me to do?"

She smiled at him. "Get dressed. I need you to help me carry two bodies." She didn't articulate they were his.

"Two?" This was the most shocked he'd seemed with anything she'd told him. "How'd that happen?"

"Yes, two." She didn't say anything further.

Neither of them spoke on the drive back to Boston. Denise had been up for more than twenty-four hours but still had the energy to do what was needed. She sat by a man she'd known for most of her life and just met. Mike finally spoke in the condo, but she did not expect it. The two of them stood over the body. She watched as Mike's eyes surveyed the head injury. He glanced at her and then back at the body. She waited for him to ask what had transpired, but he never did. Instead, he kneeled, face to face with himself.

"It's a valuable thing to understand your mortality. I was simply created, and it's easy under that pretense to not give life the weight it deserves. Seeing myself ... like this has changed that."

His comments reminded Denise how eloquent Mike could be. But she didn't need philosophy; she needed help cleaning up blood.

It was almost evening again when they pulled back into the driveway of their home. For the second time that day Mike stared at an identical corpse.

"Man, is that really how I look?" He'd come to terms with the situation. They lifted the body and carried it to the kitchen. Mike had bought them a massive pizza oven years ago. He liked the novelty of it, and the sheer size of the oven made it a good item for the overly large room. Denise had always hated it. She told Mike a million times that they would never use it. Well, he was right; now they were using it. If he were alive, he'd probably even be smug about how useful the oven had suddenly become.

As Mike and Denise prepared to toss the body, Denise shouted, "Wait!" It was not for final goodbyes. She grabbed the wedding band off the hand and unceremoniously put it on Mike's finger.

"There." They tossed the body into the oven and then the next.

Mike watched the flames dance as he closed the door. "I've died twice now, and I'm still around. Tough to get rid of me." It was the type of joke Mike would typically make, but there was a darkness to it. Denise laughed to try and soften it.

"What do we do now?" He stared at the flames. "Will people come looking for... me?"

"They won't investigate a murder that never happened, but they might try to take away your permit to keep clones. I hope this doesn't sound indelicate, but it's illegal to dispose of clones the way we did." Denise saw him mouth the word "dispose" in anger.

"There are six more of you. If they take those clones away, we'll be bankrupt… I mean it when I say 'we.'" She looked at Mike. "We're a team now. Tomorrow, you must inform them that you disposed of two clones and convince them not to investigate or charge you. Do this for us, for yourself, or our daughter. I don't care. Just do it."

Mike looked at her. "Will our daughter notice the difference?"

"Sadly, she probably won't. Mike wasn't around enough. Even I'm still uncertain if the two of you are that different."

He nodded; it seemed to bring him comfort.

The next day, Denise and Mike waited in a room for the district manager of Works. The two of them sat in silence. Denise was terrified, but Mike appeared exceptionally relaxed despite having very little context. The self-doubt she had seen previously had disappeared. He walked around the office with a bounce in his step. Mike pointed at a picture of himself and the district manager on the manager's desk. They had their arms around each other. "We don't get along at all." Mike's sarcasm was surprisingly relaxed.

"That was the Super Bowl two years ago. It's good to remember how important your business is to them. Do you remember everything I told you? Should we review it all again?"

"No. I'm good."

The manager opened the door and walked in. His name was Charles Sanders. Denise had never liked him. He had filled Mike's head with images of an empire only to sell more clones. On top of that, he was a pig.

"Mike! Good to see you." He patted Mike on the back and shook his hand. He reached across to shake Denise's hand as an afterthought.

"Charles! Always a pleasure, my friend."

"Mike, first, I want to say how happy I am that the lawsuit against your clone, and by extension yourself, was thrown out. I'd have felt terrible if we were somehow responsible for that. It's our goal here to improve your life, not make it more difficult."

Mike smiled. "I hadn't heard yet. Honestly, I always thought there was zero chance it'd hold up, so I hadn't been paying attention. I think Mr. Rytz is traveling now anyway; I wasn't planning to check in with him until his trip was done. I couldn't be seen reaching out to him while he was making his decision. Didn't want to give them any reason not to uphold it."

"Yes, I suppose I was calling that poor gentleman constantly waiting for the news. I felt as responsible as that clone. You're family here, Mike. We can't let something like that happen to our family."

Denise tried not to let her face betray surprise. "Sorry, I missed that, Charles. That verdict, when was it passed? I hadn't heard about this."

"Oh, a couple days ago. I'm sure Mike didn't want to bother you with something so unlikely." Charles winked at Mike as if doing him some big favor.

Mike turned briefly to Denise and smiled. "I didn't want you to worry. You know how we are; we always have a plan, baby." With that single acknowledgment of everything he'd caused, he turned to Charles and continued, "I appreciate you watching out for us like that. We're here, though, because I disposed of two of my clones, but it wasn't at your disposal center."

Charles's tone changed. "Mike, we've been friends for a long time, but you must get a permit to dispose of clones. Why'd you do that? There will have to be a hearing."

Mike walked around the table and touched the man's shoulders. It was such a unique Mike gesture that it gave her chills. He'd approached her like that many times. He always wanted something, and he always got it.

"You and I are very familiar with each other. I'm one of the largest private purchasers of clones, and that will not change. I don't see why disposing of them differs from cutting my fingernails. They are extensions of myself, and I pay you handsomely for them. We can continue to make both our lives great or make this incredibly difficult."

Charles spoke, but his voice was less and less confident. "Look, what would you have me do? Lie and say you disposed of the clones properly? What if there's a government investigation? If it was one clone, maybe, but why two? Why did you have to make it two? Two will turn heads."

"That's exactly what I need you to do. I agree; the second clone was foolish of me." Mike turned and looked at Denise. "I did not expect that... to happen.

But the clone in Baltimore made perfect sense. He wasn't performing as expected. I don't think anyone will question why he was decommissioned. My reputation and career were put in jeopardy. Anyone that challenges my livelihood will meet that end." Mike looked directly at Charles. There was a long silence. Denise sat there calmly, knowing that Charles would relent.

"Okay, Mike. I'll do this for you. Get out of here, and let's not speak again for some time."

Mike smiled. "If it helps, you'll notice in the system that I submitted the paperwork to get a replacement for the Baltimore clone four days ago. I noted that I would likely come this week for formal disposal. I just happened to do it myself."

Mike and Denise exited the room and walked to the car. It was over. To Denise's surprise, she felt more at peace with life than two weeks ago.

"What next?" Mike asked.

"I'm surprised you don't have it planned out."

A small smile appeared on his lips, but he didn't reply.

"We hold hands and go home," she said.

He gripped her hand. Something Mike hadn't done in years. She gripped it back.

One Simple Thing

Allison looked over at her mom. "Where should we go for lunch after?"

"You think you'll want to eat after proving ghosts are real?"

Allison smiled. "It's a stupid experiment. They all have catchy titles like that. I do these all the time for money, and half are only a survey. Maybe if I make ghost noises, we can go home early."

The mom and daughter giggled until they were interrupted by a young man walking into the room. "Please put these gowns on over your clothes, and we'll show you to your individual rooms." He tossed two gray gowns and disappeared down the hall.

Allison sat in a room that wasn't much larger than her bedroom at home. It had a single white table that held a computer. In the middle of the table was a blue light bulb, but in every other capacity, the room was barren. She sat quietly until the door opened, and an older gentleman entered and sat down.

"I'm Mr. Lawrence. I will ask you a few questions, and then you and I will be part of something groundbreaking." His hair was gray and disheveled in an almost cartoonish mad-scientist way, which matched his speech. Allison could barely take him seriously.

"Is that your mom who came with you today?"

"Of course, the ad said you needed a mother and daughter."

Mr. Lawrence simply continued with his questions. "And do you have a good relationship with your mother? Do you love her?"

"Yes. She's my best friend." Mr. Lawrence smiled slightly and wrote something in his notebook.

"I'm going to put an image on the computer that is a video feed from the room down the hall." The computer on the table now showed a feed of Allison's mom sitting across from a man in a similar room.

"Give me a second to connect the audio so you can both hear me. Molly, can you hear me?"

Allison heard her mom out of a speaker in the room. "Yes, I can hear you."

"Molly, is it fair to say that you would be willing to do anything for your daughter?"

"Yes, anything she needed."

"Excellent." He quickly scribbled something and continued. "Now that you can both hear me, I want to explain why we're here. For centuries, people have wrestled with whether there are ghosts. Some people see them. Some don't. It's arguably the greatest question, whether you can transcend the physical body, yet people treat it like a joke or sideshow attraction." He seemed visibly angry at the lack of respect that ghosts received, and Allison thought back to all her jokes in the waiting room. "Today we will change that with a genius experiment in its simplicity. The current theories, which are all unfortunately based on secondhand experiences, are that ghosts are strongest in the place of their death and when they have unfinished business. It would obviously increase the chances of a ghost if you could then combine these two things." He paused. "Molly, are you still hearing this?"

"Yes. Can still hear." Allison shifted uneasily in her chair. She didn't like being in a different room than her mother.

"Molly, we have a blue light bulb in the center of the table in our room. It is not plugged in. Do you understand?"

"Okay..."

"Molly, listen carefully. In the next minute, we are going to murder you. After your death, we are going to give you five minutes to turn the light bulb in this room on, or I will murder your daughter as well. I expect this is a clearer directive than any ghost has ever received."

Molly looked shocked and stood up. "I don't want to do this anymore." She ran to the door and pulled on the handle, but the door wasn't moving. "Let me out!" Molly banged against the door, and then the screen suddenly went black.

"What happened?" Allison screamed.

In a calm voice, Mr. Lawrence replied, "That camera appears to be down. We will go to the one in the back of the room."

He typed something into the computer, and a slightly different image appeared. It was the same room, but Allison could now only see the back of her mom's head and the feed was fuzzy. The man in the room pulled out a gun and shot her in the head. Molly fell.

Allison screamed. "No! I don't... No!" She jumped out of her chair and yelled at the computer, "Mom!"

Mr. Lawrence pulled a gun out of his coat and leveled it at her. "I know you are in shock, but I need you to focus on that light for five minutes. Watch it. Your mom might still be out there. Tell me right away if the light turns blue."

Allison was shaking and couldn't understand what was happening. It was all a blur, and before she knew it, he was looking at his watch and telling her, "Time's up." She hoped that he'd just kill her; she'd brought her mom here, and it was all her fault. Allison didn't notice the change in his tone; the entire world rang in her ears.

"I'm putting this down on the desk. Your mom is fine, and the gun is fake. It's all to see if you believe enough to see the light turn on. Ghosts aren't real, and it's perception that needs to be studied. We've had two students who saw the light turn blue, but it's tough to control if they were simply trying to appease me because of this gun. Now, next time, what I might..."

Allison didn't hear a word. She didn't care what he had to say. She lunged across the table and stabbed her pen into his neck.

He screamed and clutched his neck as blood shot out. "It's a damn test to see if you believe the light turns on."

The world came roaring back for Allison as the fog she was swimming in started to lift. Mr. Lawrence's mad scientist look appeared to be from a fake wig, now sliding down the side of his head in blood and sweat. Allison was speechless as he reached up and put his hands on her throat. "You'll pay..." His hand slowly fell as his eyes tilted back in his head.

Allison sat there in shock and solitude until the blue light slowly but surely lit up behind her.

Creo Cube

Jimmy, Colin, and Rob charged into the house. The boys were fourteen, thirteen, and twelve, respectively. It was a warm summer day, and damp heat hung in the air. The three boys ran through the expansive halls, pushing and laughing, reminiscent of the timeless way boys had played centuries ago.

"Where are your parents?" Jimmy said.

"At work. We can be as loud as we want."

The three boys, especially Colin, were tired after they ran home from school. Colin was considerably smaller despite being of the same age as the other two boys.

"This house is amazing. You're so lucky!" Jimmy was in awe as the boys walked from room to room.

"Isn't it great?" said Rob. "Mr. Turner's family owned it. Our gym teacher. The games room is awesome."

"Let's play!" Colin piped up.

As the boys turned to Colin, they noticed him eating candy from his backpack. The other boys stood mesmerized as they watched.

"Where's the Creo Cube? I want some candy." Jimmy had not taken his eyes off Colin's candy.

"In the kitchen."

The boys ran toward the kitchen, and Colin slowly followed. Now that his mouth was full, he was making less noise than the others.

The three of them entered the kitchen and walked toward the center of the room, where the Creo Cube was the focal point. It was a beautiful box of silver and black, slightly larger than historical ovens. The sleek edges surrounded an empty interior as it waited for instructions.

Jimmy stood at the control panel on the side. "Colin, what's that candy?" It seemed an eternity for the boys as Colin finally stopped smacking his lips long enough to answer.

"Sugar Rockets," replied Colin. He was now keenly focused on the next piece held in his hand.

Jimmy searched for Sugar Rockets in the Creo Cube index. A couple of seconds passed before he kicked the cube in frustration. "This didn't come with Sugar Rockets loaded!"

Colin spoke up. "You never loaded these? It's easy."

"Never. You know how?"

"Yeah, I can't believe I haven't told you! This is the funniest story. I was messing around with the school's Creo Cube last week. I put a rat inside the cube and loaded it in as a hair scrunchie. I watched as the girls at school went to get a scrunchie, picked it on the menu, and then suddenly a giant rat would appear."

"That's unbelievable," Jimmy laughed. The three boys couldn't contain their giggles.

"I bet some of them still grabbed it before realizing," Rob said. "You get in trouble?"

"Mr. Turner yelled at me in front of the girls. But after they left, he said he and his friends used to play with the cubes when they were younger, too. He thought it was funny."

Jimmy was still laughing, but Rob had gone silent. He stared intently at the cube. "Do you think anyone has ever gone in?"

"I don't know, but we should," said Colin. Imagine if we programmed ourselves in as dinner, and then when our parents ordered it, we surprised them."

"Let's try!" said Rob. Rob was always the first to try anything and attempted to climb in. After a minute of struggling, it was apparent that he was far too large.

"I think Colin is probably the only one that fits," Jimmy said.

Now that it would be Colin, he seemed to have lost some of his earlier enthusiasm for testing the cube. He nodded solemnly at the others and started to climb in. It took him a while to make himself fit, and for a moment, it seemed as if he would have preferred he didn't. He shifted his legs up to his chest so they could finally close the screen on the front. The two other boys now stood over him. They entered the name of this new item in the index as "COLIN." Colin gave them a small wave with only his fingers in the little bit of room that remained.

“Should we press it on the count of three?” said Rob.

“Yes,” replied Jimmy. “Okay, one, two, three.”

They pressed the button. Colin disappeared in a flash of light. It was all very simple and clean except for what sounded like a small scream. It was audible for only an instant and then nothing. The two boys looked at each other. Neither was willing to say what they had just heard and give truth to it.

“Let’s get him back,” said Jimmy. The boys were noticeably nervous as Colin's absence was acute. Jimmy quickly thumbed the index until it reached “COLIN.” He pressed the button; the cube flashed briefly, and then Colin was back in the box. A massive grin appeared on his face as he looked around.

“Unbelievable!” Jimmy and Rob laughed and hugged each other. “You went and came back!” Rob shouted at Colin as he helped him out of the cube.

“What was it like?” asked Jimmy.

Colin slowly got his bearings and hugged the two of them, giggling. “It was quick. It was only a flash, and then I was back. I thought you were lying when you said I had left, but I noticed you were suddenly standing in different spots.”

The boys laughed and jumped up and down. As with all young boys, the excitement quickly faded as they wondered what was next.

“Games room now?” Rob finally said.

The boys nodded and ran out of the room. The cube stood clean and shimmering in the center of the room. The word “COLIN” remained illuminated on the index.

—— «» ——

Colin felt the light and heat immediately. It was extremely painful for an instant, and then he couldn’t feel it anymore; he couldn’t feel much of anything anymore. He looked around and blinked as his eyes adjusted. It appeared he was in a white room. There was nothing around him. He wondered if this was where items went before people ordered them back from the cube. Suddenly, a tiny shape appeared before him. It was headed toward him. He couldn’t make it out. Perhaps these were workers coming to get him to go back. As the image got closer, he noticed it was a small boy. The boy must have been only slightly younger than he was. His legs were moving as quickly as possible as he ran toward Colin. He stopped a foot in front of Colin and faced him. Before Colin could ask him anything, the little boy eagerly put his hand out. "I'm Dave Turner. Are you here to take me home?"

Colin didn't recognize the boy, but he recognized his eyes; he saw them every day at school. "Mr. Turner, is that you?" The boy looked at Colin and didn't understand. His eyes were tearing up.

"Mr. Turner is my dad… Do you know him? It feels like I haven't seen him in forever."

Companion

Day 42

I floated into the main compartment and asked the computer to put my course on screen. There was no one else to ask. It would be two years of this before I returned to the outer system. Humanity had never explored this far. On two separate occasions, people got close but never made the entire trip. It was a weird thing I had been tasked with; I was headed toward an area of space where, by all accounts, there was nothing. The target presented no gravitational anomalies, nothing that emitted light, and no impact on the universe. Based on the readings, it was an exceptionally dull place. I was headed there because it hadn't always been that way. Decades ago, satellites could see gravity being emitted from this single point. As soon as organizations started sending probes, nothing could be found, as if an entire part of the universe had turned itself off. It was like seeing someone make a face out of the corner of your eye. Any response, especially one aimed at concealment, was a sign of intelligent life. That's why I was here, to find nothing. It was an expedition that had been difficult to explain to the scientific community and even more difficult to explain to my wife.

Day 47

I often spoke to myself to pass the time. I would reminisce about books I'd read or places I'd visited. Many times, I talked about Amanda as if I was telling a new friend about my true love. Friends often get sick of hearing how in love you are, and the ship was no different, except that it couldn't protest. I could talk for hours about the streets of Paris. Amanda and I had gone when we were young, and I let my mind take me back. Talking to myself was a natural way to deal with the solitude and the computer, and I agreed that it was not because I was going crazy. Before this trip, I'd been sure I enjoyed solitude; it allowed me to recharge from the artificial interactions that make up a person's day. But without that variability, I was less and less sure that my own company was best.

Day 52

There was a brief window every several days where I could message my wife instantaneously; a period when the signal was no longer interrupted by celestial bodies. We could send emails the rest of the time, but it wasn't the same. Each communication window was diligently set on my watch and instruments. I planned my days around it, and a channel was about to become available. I sat at the terminal and waited for the light to notify me the channel was open. My watch calculated that the channel should be opening. Usually, I was exactly right, and I took pride in that, but this time, it appeared I was off by a few seconds. As if in response to my concerns, the light turned on. After all that anticipation, I didn't know what to type. My days were all the same. What could I possibly share with her?

Me: Hi!

Amanda: John! How's the day?

Me: Good. I studied and worked through some calibrations. You?

Amanda: Look at us being so productive. I have a list of things I want to complete before you return.

Me: That's exciting! Make sure you leave me some chores.

Amanda: Don't worry, your chores are still progressing at the same pace as when you were home...

Me: Haha. I'm still planning to unload the dishwasher like I said I would the night before I left. It's just that I've been working late for the past twelve hundred and forty hours. That's the number of hours I've been away...

Amanda: Yes, John. You're very smart. That's some complex astronaut math, but I managed to understand it.

Me: I miss you. What do you want to complete while I'm gone?

Amanda: I'd like to run a marathon and learn to box. That's all I have so far. You'll need to give me more time to think of other ones... I will need you to give me at least a few years.

I laughed. The sound felt out of place on the ship.

Me: I can do that... I miss how funny you are.

Amanda: You're plenty funny. Does the computer laugh at your jokes?

Me: Nope. Unfortunately, it is quite an advanced AI. Much more intelligent than that.

Day 60

Me: Have you thought of any more goals for yourself while I'm away?

Amanda: Yes! Several new ones. I want to get involved with a charity and learn a new language. Most importantly, though, I want to see Paris. I've read so much about it, and everyone mentions it to the point that it seems as if a part of living is to spend some time there.

I looked at the screen to make sure I was reading correctly.

Me: Paris? We've been to Paris. How can you forget?

Amanda: I was only joking. I remember! It was magical.

The light flashed above the screen, meaning the connection would soon be interrupted.

Me: We're going to lose our connection. I love you so much!

Amanda: I love you too! We'll go to Paris again when you return.

The light darkened. She was gone. How could she forget Paris? Was she forgetting me? I was thankful for the background hum of the life support systems. It was comforting to hear something other than my thoughts.

Day 65

Amanda and I were barely talking. Whenever I tried to speak to her about something meaningful, she told me she had to go and that I should focus on the mission. I feared we were drifting apart. Before the mission, we'd told each other that neither of us should worry about the other and that our love would survive, regardless of what the distance made us feel. Whether she believed that or not, she'd loved me enough to let me go. Love like that should prevent any doubts I harbored, but I found that, without holding her or being with her, I questioned what I knew about us and her. All I had were words on a screen.

Day 74

I finished all my daily calibrations early because I knew a window was approaching. I sat at the terminal, waiting for the light.

Me: How're you?

Amanda: I'm good. Raining here unfortunately.

Me: I almost envy that. There's no change here; the environment is constant. Variety is a gift.

Amanda: I'm sorry. How's your studying progressing?

Me: Good. Moving through it steadily.

Amanda: Are the gravity intervals annoying?

Me: Yes! They're so painful and tiring! Just the other day...

I stopped typing. I'd never told Amanda about the gravity intervals. Every day, I had to work out in a chamber that simulated increased gravity. It kept my body strong over a long journey, but it always felt as if I was suffocating. I'd screamed in the chamber only a few days ago. Amanda wouldn't know this. Had the computer told her? Were people updating her so she could provide psychological support?

Me: I'm actually going to go Amanda. I'm tired.

Amanda: Okay!

There was nowhere to go.

Day 90

I hadn't known what to do or how to act for the last week. The last time a window for conversation came up, I pretended I was busy. I wondered if maybe I'd told Amanda about the intervals and forgot. Was I simply paranoid after months without human contact? I'd read about this happening, but I always thought I was immune and had a unique strength. I suppose everyone likes to feel they're special. On the first trip, a pilot blew a hole in his ship. There was never an explanation, but the unspoken consensus had been that he was mentally weak. I wasn't going to let that be me. I was imagining problems that weren't there.

Day 110

The light was on. Asking me to come talk.

Me: Amanda! Sorry, I've been distant lately. I was struggling for a bit.

Amanda: What was wrong?

Me: I was having difficulty with loneliness. It impacted me more than I thought. I was disappointed with myself and embarrassed.

Amanda: You're better now?

Me: Yes! Being away is an interesting thing; it helps you understand what you value. I am very excited to see you again. A little less than two years now!

Amanda: Two years? Your trip is eight.

I stared at the screen.

Me: Are you joking? Why'd you say that?

Amanda: You signed up for an eight-year term. I don't understand what you're saying.

I was almost blind now with fear and anger. I was not out here for another eight years. I was on a two-year term. Only a few days ago I'd double-checked our progress. I shouted for the computer to put our latest course on the screen. It popped up. It was different. I didn't go through the details but stared only at the top right corner. It read: *Expected duration: Eight years and twenty days.* My hands shook as I started typing.

Me: Who am I talking to right now?!

Amanda: You're sounding crazy, and it's scaring me. What's happening up there?

Me: I know it isn't you!

Amanda: This isn't you! You're smarter than this. You sound as if you're getting all confused out there! I know it must be tough. You can talk to me about anything. Remember when we explored that cave in the Rocky Mountains when we were young and foolish.

I paused and thought about it.

Me: I remember.

Amanda: Remember you were scared to get to the other side of the cave, and I told you to trust me. We made it out the other end. This will be the same, even if you must turn back. You will get out of this cave one way or another.

Only Amanda knew about the cave.

Me: You're right. Why'd you say turn back, though? What are they saying about the voyage on the news? Believe me, I've thought about it, but I can't turn back. We've tried this journey twice already. I don't think we'd get funding a fourth time. I believe in this trip. We need to find out if we are not alone in this universe.

As I was typing, my watch beeped. It noted that a window for conversation was ten minutes away. I knew that I couldn't have been this far off on my calculations. There was no window with Earth based on our current alignment, and there was certainly no connection with Amanda. I watched as text continued to populate the screen.

Amanda: Why's it so important for you to visit this place? Maybe some things should be left alone.

Capital Markets

"The Market creates an equality that humanity has always desired but never experienced before. The Market doesn't care who you are or what you have done; it is available to everyone and impacts everyone. It is perfect, without restrictions, as nature intended."

— President Hyde

Christian thought he was going to puke. It was all hitting him in a wave. He opened the Market on his console. His hands shook as he typed his citizen number and clicked on his profile. The bid on his life had ticked up once more and now totaled four million. It could only be increased by a hundred thousand each day, giving him ten more days before it would eclipse what he was worth. He wondered if he would try to run or simply surrender. His boss walked by his console as he tried to fathom what was happening entirely. He tried to minimize the Marketplace, but it was too late; his boss had noticed. "I don't pay you to sit around bidding all day. I need that analysis by this aft."

Christian stammered. "Yes, sir." A minute before, he had been trying to find his boss, and now he suddenly felt sheepish. As Mr. Kelly started to walk away, he finally called out, "Can I talk to you later, sir? Privately. It's important."

"Sure, as long as you get those reports done. When you submit them, come on over to my office, and we can chat."

Christian had never worked so hard in his life. The reports were completed in an hour. He submitted them and walked down the hall to Mr. Kelly's office. He knocked once, no reply. He paced and knocked again. Justin from accounting walked down the hall and quickly nodded before averting his eyes. Christian stared at his back as he walked away. He was running out of time. In desperation, Christian opened the door and barged into the office.

Mr. Kelly was sitting in his chair with his virtual reality headset on. To get his attention, Christian slammed the door behind him. Mr. Kelly ripped the headset off in a fluster.

"Sorry, your door was open," said Christian. "I've submitted those reports."

Mr. Kelly looked as if he had much to say but finally settled on, "Please sit down."

Christian sat down, and the two men looked at each other. Mr. Kelly was nice enough, but he was not the type to ask what was wrong. Christian blurted out, "Someone has almost bid up to my murder threshold."

Mr. Kelly raised his eyebrows and sat up straight. "Really? It isn't a prank or something? A real bid for life is so rare in the professional world. What is your ascribed value?"

"Five million."

"Why so low? The present value of your earnings here must be at least ten million."

"I have a lot of debt from when I was younger. I made..." Christian looked down. "I made some foolish decisions. I don't have any kids either, so I don't have any future value from them."

"Do you know the person bidding you up?"

"Some multimillionaire named Ryan Del. He thinks I was trying to sleep with his girlfriend."

"Were you?" Mr. Kelly leaned forward in his chair. He was increasingly interested now that both murder and sex were involved.

"Not after I found out he's worth two hundred million."

Despite the gravity of the situation, a small laugh was shared between the two men.

"What if you do this? Try to get close to his wife, and then get her to convince him to change his mind." Another laugh was shared.

There was a longer pause before Mr. Kelly spoke again. "Listen, that is upsetting, but I don't know what I can do. Even if I was willing to pledge you, it sounds as if he would just bid me up as well. I can't risk that... Maybe he is only trying to scare you and will never submit an amount above your worth. It could just be a warning?"

Christian shook his head. "No, he's different. He isn't rational." He added, in a whisper, "One thing you could do is submit a raise for me to head office. You would never have to pay for it. It would only be so that it is factored into the calculations in the Marketplace. I need more time, which would get it for me."

Mr. Kelly almost exploded at the notion. "Do you not believe in the free marketplace? Look, I'm sorry for what's happening to you, but this country was built on the free market. There's a price for everything and if people want to create incremental value, regardless of what they want to do, we need to support it. Your life is only worth five million. If this guy is willing to pay the government six million to kill you, don't you think they should take it? Think of how much good they could do with that extra money. All the sick kids they could help. All the research they could afford. It is more than you'll do for the world. That's how they measure it. Look, I'm sorry this is happening to you, but this is the world we live in. We are a big company, and we can't interfere in other people's transactions. Not only is it policy, but if we get pulled into something, it could bankrupt us, especially if someone is willing to throw their weight around. Susan had a hospital put a claim on all her kid's earnings from a recent operation, and they lost their house. We wanted to help but couldn't. There is something new every day."

Christian couldn't stomach the absurdity. "People shouldn't be able to buy a life simply because they are putting more money into the system! Why am I only worth five million? There shouldn't be a market for everything!"

"Because that's what your life is worth! Look, you could have worked harder, you could have had kids, you could have contributed more, but you didn't. Everyone loves the Marketplace until they don't. I know why you have all that debt. Do you think I didn't read your file? You were distracted and ran that kid over. It was a tragedy and an accident, but you still would have gone to jail, given the speed you were going. You paid the market rate to society to get out of your sentence. That's fine. I wouldn't have hired you if I didn't think that was appropriate, but you can't suddenly fight the system. You would be rotting in jail if you were around sixty years ago before the Marketplace existed."

Christian was shaking. "Go to hell. I think about that accident every day, but I can't go back. It happened, and it was final. There was no changing that. All that could happen was that everyone impacted continued with their lives and tried to contribute, including myself. Here, there is a chance, but you are condemning me. If I survive, I will make sure you get yours." He spat on the floor.

"I'm calling security. Also, I will be docking your go-forward pay the normal amount for this indiscretion. You probably aren't very good with math, so I'll tell you right now; that gives you five days with your new go-forward present value."

Christian walked back to his desk and grabbed his coat. The exchange with his boss had awoken a fire in him, affirming his desire to survive. He grabbed his phone and looked for possible drivers outside the office building. He scrolled past the five-star and four-star ratings. He scrolled almost to the very bottom. People only chose drivers over automatic vehicles for two reasons these days: they were going to a lovely cottage with rural roads that the auto wasn't familiar with, or they didn't want the autopilot tracking where they went. Today, he was the latter. He needed someone with a non-traditional mentality; someone who had been to where he was going. In five minutes, a driver named Raphael pulled up. He had a worn face and gray stubble. His face was cast in shadows thanks to the hat of a hockey team that no longer existed.

"Afternoon, I need you to take me to the center of the Market. Not the financial district. The beating heart of it, and not the outskirts where you take bachelor parties and someone with a midlife crisis. I need serious money."

Raphael smiled in the rearview mirror. "And good afternoon to you."

"I'm serious."

Raphael turned around in his seat and looked Christian up and down. "You won't survive there."

Christian tried to sound confident, more for himself than Raphael. "I'll figure something out. Are you going to take me there or not?"

Raphael didn't respond as he flipped through a virtual screen on the front windshield.

"Are you looking at my position on the Marketplace?!"

"It's a three-hour drive. Sometimes, people try this on their last day and don't even have enough money to cover the trip. You look good. Here we go."

The car pulled out into the uniform flow of traffic, which started to thin out as they reached the city's outskirts. It was early evening, and the light was fading, but a new light was starting to replace it on the horizon. As they drove, a dull glow of lights, furnaces, engines, and fires was rising ahead of them. They started to pass refineries, processing plants, cell phone towers, gravel mines, and other industrial behemoths that the wealthy of the city had simply paid to have relocated further away from their yards. They started to pass bars and clubs where enough money would let you do anything. There was a constant hum, an energy, in the air.

Raphael slowed down to point at a flashing sign that said they were approaching the orange line. "I assume you didn't come all this way to stop at the orange line?" The car stopped, and the two stared across a twenty-meter gap without buildings or light. On the other side of this darkness, they could see the outlines of buildings in the dust and individuals milling around. The hum of industry had been replaced by shouts and screams. A man walked out of the gap carrying a sac over one shoulder. He was covered in blood and did not raise his head to make eye contact.

"Cross the orange line."

"As you wish." Raphael switched into drive and rolled the car forward.

The mandatory warning blared on the car's computer. "*Be aware that you are crossing the orange line. Crime is permitted if the required toll is paid immediately. Emergency services will not respond in this area unless the toll for high-risk emergency response is paid. We appreciate your support of the economy.*"

The car crept across the expanse. Christian was staring out the window, trying to make out shapes in the shadows, when the driver's voice boomed, "You must give me someplace to go, man! We're sitting ducks." The driver put his foot on the gas and started them off in one direction before waiting for guidance.

Christian stammered. "Uh, right, what would you suggest?"

"Look. Here are your options for the money you want. You could pay a drug company to experiment on you. It's not enough cash, though, and if it is enough cash, it means it will most likely kill you. You can do the back-and-forth trade and have someone pay you here to do something for them back in the city, but I don't think anyone ever gets away with that. I will be honest, your best bet is a fighting ring. They like putting two greenhorns against each other so you can get a matchup quickly. You could make enough every few days to stay ahead of this. Maybe."

"Okay." Christians wrung his hands. "Can you take me there?"

"That's where we're going."

After a couple more minutes, they pulled up beside what looked like a concrete box. A thin blue line outlined the main walls, making them visible against the darkness. That single light was the equivalent of a sign out here.

Raphael stopped in front but didn't put the car in park. "You go in there. Tell them you are looking for whatever matchup will pay the most. Don't get worked up about who you are against. It will be someone like you. The fights last longer that way."

"Okay. Thanks for the advice." Christian transferred the money and started to exit the vehicle.

"Do you want me to wait and run the meter? It can sometimes be hours before you get a car out here to take you back."

Christian gave a dejected "No." The man was resigned to his fate.

As Christian walked away, Raphael called out, "Remember, even if you have nothing else, you have the fact you are fighting for your life. Some guys come out here because they want to buy a new car or a new watch. That difference should carry you."

"And what if I find myself looking at someone else fighting for their life?"

"Well... then, you are."

Raphael drove away into the darkness.

Christian approached the door as a massive shadow of a man emerged from the wall. His voice sounded like gravel.

"It's one hundred bucks to watch. You are lucky, it's all death matches tonight."

"Lucky... I'm actually looking to fight." The bouncer looked him up and down and then whispered something into an earpiece.

"Okay." He pushed against a door behind him with his massive hand. "Take your first left and tell the lady you want to fight."

Christian nodded and walked through the dark hallway. A tall woman in a long leather jacket waited at the end.

"I'm supposed to talk to you."

She barely looked at him while she spoke. "Can you go now?"

"What?"

"Can you fight now? We had someone drop out that was a similar size. It's simple: you can or can't. Don't waste my time. You win, we will give you three hundred thousand dollars."

"And if I lose?"

She stared at him. "Then it doesn't matter."

"I'll do it." His hands were shaking with adrenaline.

"Okay. We need a photo for identification. Then just walk through this hallway to the left and down the hall for Arena One."

"Thanks. And then what?"

"And then you survive... or you don't." It was the first time she had smiled.

Christian walked down the hall. The ground was covered in blood, and his nostrils filled with the metallic smell of it. He turned toward Arena One and could already hear the chant of the crowd. His heart pounded. He stopped at the threshold of the arena and then stepped inside. The large ceiling lights were blinding, but he got his bearings. The arena was circular, with a narrow wall that separated the crowd. He couldn't make out faces, but he heard them shouting and screaming. In the far corner, behind a fence, he could make out a ragtag group likely made up of waiting fighters. His eyes focused on cages containing various animals when he noticed he was not alone in the arena. A thin man, probably ten years his junior, was crouched at the opposite end. He was going to ask what happened next, but the man's stance left him with no questions. He couldn't believe where he was, but he had no time to think about it as the man charged toward him.

The man tackled him around the waist, but Christian used the man's momentum to throw him past. The man quickly regained his footing and tackled him again, this time wrapping both arms around Christian's torso and ripping him to the ground. Christian kicked him off and stood up. The man leveled a kick right into Christian's left leg from the ground. The sharp pain made him worry it was broken, but he stumbled and was able to put a bit of weight on it. It would do. The pain focused his senses entirely.

Christian now stood across from him, knowing the man would charge him again. When he did, Christian ducked and launched the man over his back. Christian quickly turned and tried to put his foot down on the man's head, but he rolled. Christian let his momentum carry him forward and fell with his second leg, led by his knee, into the man's back. He hit hard and knocked the air out of the man. With his knee on his back, Christian used it as leverage to grab the man's left arm. He pulled the arm until he felt it snap. The man was no longer writhing beneath him with the same energy, and there was now an inevitableness to the fight.

Christian rolled him over and put both hands around his neck. The man punched Christian with his remaining arm, but the blows slowed. Christian reached out with his right hand to grab a rock. He paused as he raised the rock above the man's head; he thought about watching his favorite TV shows in his apartment only a couple of weeks ago. His left hand was held firmly around the man's neck, and he was squirming less and less. The man sensed his brief pause and started to speak.

"My brother is going to die."

"I don't care!" spat Christian.

He tightened his hand, but the man's strained voice continued. "A man named Mr. Del... he... Del will..."

Christian stopped. "Ryan Del?" His blood was pounding, but his thoughts tried to push through, suggesting another way.

"Yes..."

He slowly released his grip on the man's throat. "That's the same man who is bidding me up... I'm going to let you up now. Let's think about this for a second."

The man nodded and slowly got to his feet. Christian rose beside him but couldn't put much weight on his left leg. The crowd was booing, but Christian started to shout above them, particularly toward the waiting fighters. "How many of you need Ryan Del dead?"

The room was quieter, clearly interested, and about a quarter of the people raised their hands. He gave a small smile toward the man he had almost killed. He turned back to the crowd. "And how many here would be interested in jointly bidding on Ryan Del's life?" Nearly half raised their hands. Christian turned to the other fighter. "We can work with this."

Auto

Derek leaned in close. "You ever tried it?"

This was the second time Derek had asked during class. Connor relented. "Of course not."

"Why not?"

"For starters, you get expelled. Why don't you try it?" Connor had now missed what the teacher had said. He was stressed for exams and didn't need Derek distracting him.

Derek replied in his usual voice; he had one volume. "I won't be eighteen before finals. I would be on it if I were. I bet half the kids in here are on Auto."

"Shhhh!" The word hung in the air as if Derek had hit a gong. Sitting in front of them, Rebecca turned around and gave the boys wide eyes. She was opening her mouth to say something when the bell rang.

Connor jumped out of his seat and ran to his locker. He needed to find his chemistry textbook for the next period. Connor dumped his backpack on the ground to see if he'd packed it and forgot. All he found was Derek, suddenly beside him again.

"Look, Connor, I'm happy to have drinks on my porch for the next forty years. But I know you want to escape this town. Half the kids in school will be on Auto for exams, and I don't know why you'd disadvantage yourself. That's all. Sorry, I stressed you out." Derek smiled and walked away. It was one of the few times Connor had seen Derek finish talking by choice. Connor shook his head and collected his books. He still hadn't found his chemistry textbook.

That night, he tossed and turned, unable to sleep.

The next day, Connor approached Derek in the halls. "What exactly does Auto do?"

Derek put his arm around Connor as if seeing an old friend for the first time in years. "Now you're talking! It shuts down parts of your mind and focuses only on one specific task. For example, I bet right now you're thinking a little about class, a little about lunch, and a little about the girls' volleyball team. Imagine how you'd do on exams if all that brain power were directed toward studying?"

"What if I still want to think about the girls' volleyball team?"

Derek laughed. Connor shifted his weight back and forth. "Have you heard of the problems?"

"What problems?"

"My dad told me that when he was in the army, a friend of his died because of Auto. He made me promise never to use it or even mention it. He returned from his tour a year ago, but it isn't the same. Sometimes, I'll find him standing in the middle of a room. He won't be doing anything, but he could stand there all day. Like he's not sure how to live now."

"I'm sure the war messed everyone up, but Auto killing someone sounds like a story parents use to keep their kids from doing it. You won't believe it, but I have a class I need to get to." Derek headed down the hall. Suddenly, he turned around, pointed, and shouted, "Connor, do it!"

Connor covered his face as people turned. Derek shouted again at the hallway full of students, "What, he's having sex with people and stuff like that!"

Connor had to laugh.

Connor waited in a private appointment room at the Auto clinic the following afternoon. He'd almost lost his nerve when the doctor finally entered the room.

"Hello. I understand you're interested in Auto for exams."

"Hi," was all Connor could muster.

"Don't be nervous. You're doing nothing wrong. The school board's views on Auto haven't caught up. Do you know ninety percent of military professionals go on Auto? They simply come in here and then wake up as if nothing happened. On Auto, they're one hundred percent focused. I think it's reckless not to be on Auto for the most important things in life. If it's good enough for our servicemen and women, you know you can't be doing anything wrong."

Connor was still nervous. "Don't some of those people die on Auto? It's scary to think you can go to sleep here and then die, never knowing what happened."

The doctor became severe. "I promise you that Auto is the best version of ourselves. If you can't survive a war on Auto, you'd have died much earlier without it. For your exams, it will enhance your existing skills. A smart kid like you will simply do better. Have you signed the waiver?"

Connor reached onto the table and picked up the electronic pad. He signed it, but instead of passing it to the doctor, he held it against his chest. "What if my Auto doesn't want to study? What if it skips school or does something bad?"

"The medicine controls what you do. There's no other option for your mind." The doctor reached for the pad, and Connor released it.

"Excellent. Now, beyond the risks on the waiver, be aware that you won't remember anything. You sleep in this chair, and then, after your exams, Auto will bring you back here."

"Why don't people remember anything?"

"It's complicated, but I'll give you the simple answer. A brain on Auto is devoting all mental capacity to the primary task we pick. In the army, for example, the focus is survival. For you, it's doing well in your exams. The mind has no additional room to store memories."

This hardly alleviated Connor's concern. "Am I the same person on Auto or different?"

"You're the same person but with different priorities. No one can even tell the difference." He started scanning through Connor's file and summarizing the procedure. "The only invasive part, beyond the serum, is a microchip we insert in your right forearm. This allows us to program when you return. The microchip then deactivates Auto. After your exams, Auto will bring you back here and turn it off. We then remove the chip. The cost includes minor plastic surgery, so you don't even get a scar during or after. Now..." The doctor trailed off.

Connor waited for him to collect his thoughts. Finally, the man looked him in the eye and said, "I'm sorry about your father."

The comment shocked Connor. His father was at work, and the room suddenly felt very cold. "What do you mean?"

"It says here your father took Auto in the military but went MIA. He never returned here."

Connor didn't know what to say. The doctor must be mistaken, but a cold sweat covered him. He suddenly wanted to get far away.

"Sorry for bringing it up; I was just surprised, given all your questions. We appreciate his sacrifice."

"It's fine. I have to run, though. Something came up." Connor stumbled over his words and exited the room. His legs were heavy as he ran the entire way home.

Connor sat at the kitchen table with his textbooks out. He was pretending to study but was just waiting for his dad to come home. He needed to talk to him. It was all he could think about. How could his dad warn him against Auto when he had used it himself? Connor thought about what a hypocrite the man was. Anger was building inside him.

It was early evening when his father suddenly barged into the house. The door slammed against the wall in a show of force that was not typical for the man.

"Where were you today? The school called and said you missed last period." There was a fire in his father's eyes that Connor hadn't seen before.

"I had to do something." Connor's voice was shaky. He didn't understand why his dad was so angry about a skipped period. It was Connor who deserved to be angry. A part of him was happy to see emotion from his father, happy to see him being a father. It reminded Connor of how things were before the war.

Connor worked up the courage to say it. "You lied to me. You took Auto during the war."

"How'd you hear that?"

"I went there myself to take some for exams. That's where I was! They said you took some when you were in the army."

His dad's expression changed.

"I'm sorry I didn't tell you. Is that all they said?"

Connor was about to reply when he looked closely at the large scar on his dad's right forearm. Connor had never examined it before. It had come back with him from the war, along with all his baggage. He remembered the doctor pointing to the same spot on his arm that afternoon. This didn't resemble the seamless outbound procedure the doctor had shown him; instead, it looked like something had been torn out. His dad noticed him looking. The warm spring air hung thick between them.

"You're still on Auto, aren't you?"

His dad now stood across from him at the table. Connor was nervous and stood up.

"You're a kid. You don't understand."

"You need to go back there and get it shut off. You aren't my father. You stole him from me."

"Connor, I'm still your father. If I go back, they kill the man I am right now. Who I am today ceases to exist. I just want to live."

"I don't care. I want my dad back! The man you have trapped inside of you!" Connor looked at his cell phone on the kitchen counter. He wouldn't be able to reach it in time. The man he had thought was his father suddenly ran around the table; Connor barely escaped his reach. Connor bounded up the stairs and locked his bedroom door. He quickly hid in a crawl space behind the bed. He could hear the man taking the stairs two at a time, and then he threw himself against the door. The door splintered. He was tearing the room apart in his search for Connor. In his head, Connor repeated that this wasn't his father. The noise outside the crawl space was getting close, but Connor wasn't afraid anymore. He only had pity in his heart, for the day someone would wake his father and tell him what had happened. He and his dad were both helpless.

Fear Class

"The full block today is scheduled for fear class. I know it's not enjoyable, but it's critical to your long-term health. I had my annual fear implant just a few days ago. The anticipation is the worst part; you will feel much better once it's behind you. Now, everyone, please clear all activities on your implants, as you are required to listen to the upcoming agreement. You will then need to consent before the exercise begins."

Jeremy sat in the back. His hands were tightly clenched in his lap as Mr. Moreau reviewed the description. He hated fear class. He promised himself that once he graduated from university, he would make enough money so that he never had to do it again. He had read about wealthy people who had entirely chosen to forgo their annual fear class. He knew that he shouldn't be truly scared and that it served an important function, but his experiences differed from those of other kids. His classmate Cynthia found herself in a plane crash, and it was over in a few minutes. Myles was hiking in his last year and got chased by a bear, which Myles thought was fantastic since it let him see a bear up close. Jeremy felt his were... real. There was a darkness to them, not just a threat but a more profound evil. Mr. Moreau drew his attention back to the front as he continued.

"Please be aware that if you do not participate in the exercise at least once a year, your health insurance will be voided. To this extent, extreme stimuli and the resulting release of adrenaline are required parts of life for a healthy individual. Let's get started." Mr. Moreau started walking between each of the chairs in the room and began activating the process on his pad.

Jeremy's close friend Reed could sense his discomfort and leaned in. "For mine, I will probably wake up and find out I'm married and have kids. Talk about horrific." Reed's girlfriend rolled her eyes as he chuckled. Jeremy would have laughed, but all he could think about was whether he would sprint out of the room. His teacher had already made it to him.

"Jeremy, are you ready?"

Jeremy paused. His legs felt like lead, and he knew he wouldn't run. "Can you see what we are going to see?"

"No, the computer does it. I have no control."

"Do you know where the computer gets the simulations from? Who creates these stories?"

"It sifts through several preprogrammed events that illicit a fight or flight response."

Jeremy knew that couldn't be true. He thought back to what he had seen last time. Mr. Moreau could see how stressed Jeremy was. He put his hand on Jeremy's shoulder and tried to calm him. "A couple of decades ago, people were constantly dying of stress-related diseases. Their bodies and minds couldn't distinguish between a real threat and something mundane like a work meeting. The lack of real external stimulus was putting them constantly on edge, and it was making them sick. The human body, our ancestors, was designed to have a couple of big stresses, a predator, or a fight with a competing tribe, and then for that instinct to be dormant until the next threat. That's what we are doing here; a big shock once a year is good for you."

Jeremy nodded. "I know... I give my consent."

Jeremy suddenly found himself walking home. He was lucid, but there was a progression to his actions that wasn't entirely his own. He entered the house as the sun was setting outside. Closing the door behind him, he called up the stairs in case anyone was home. No reply. He wanted to leave the house but knew that's where he was supposed to be. He locked the door and moved a chair into the hallway to sit and watch the door. He sat there for twenty minutes. Maybe it would be a simple burglary or a fire. He went into the kitchen to see if there were any candles. There wasn't a CREO Cube, so he turned on the oven, hoping that that might lead to the simulation there. He sat back down and wondered if a burglar was already in the house. He walked upstairs through the dark hallway and individually turned the lights on in each room. He wanted something to jump out at him and urged them to. He wanted this over with.

"Come on!" he shouted as he opened the last door. Nothing.

Jeremy went back down the stairs, leaving each light on for comfort. He sat in the chair, facing the door, and waited. The hours ticked by. Maybe he would just wait out the night and then look for something in the morning. Perhaps it was too difficult to scare him like this. That idea brought him some comfort; before he knew it, he drifted off. He awoke suddenly. The house was dark. He was terrified as he wondered what had woken him up. Why were the lights out? He didn't want to be in the house anymore. He ran to the door, fumbled with the lock, opened it, and ran out onto the street. There was no moon tonight, but being outside still provided some light. Something felt wrong. He needed to talk to someone immediately.

"Hello!" he shouted. "I'm done! I want out!" The street was silent.

He ran to his neighbor's house and pounded on the door. The door swung open; it had not been locked. Jeremy wanted to leave, but he knew he was supposed to be there.

"Hello?" he called out. He flipped the light switch, but nothing happened. Maybe it was a kidnapping or something and he was supposed to interrupt it. He heard a small voice call out "help" from upstairs.

It wasn't the intonation you would expect from a scared little kid, but he followed it anyway. He knew the trap that awaited him. Jeremy took the stairs slowly, one by one, in the darkness. He could only manage to keep one eye open out of fear. His feet were slow as he walked down the hallway on the upper floor. He went back and forth between paralyzing helplessness and wondering if there were possible ways out. In his mind, he was going to shout out, scream, to let it know that it couldn't hurt him. He wanted to let it know that he grew less and less afraid every year. He wanted to do all those things, but no sound came out. At the end of the hallway, he pushed open the door. A little boy lay bleeding on the floor. He had been cut across the gut. There was no need to see this, Jeremy thought. Why would this be here? The little boy reached out to him. As he stepped forward to help the boy, he saw the movement from behind the door. The man was wearing a goat mask and lunged toward him, swinging a knife. He grabbed Jeremy and, with his other hand, danced the knife across his stomach. Jeremy screamed as he felt his guts spill out.

"Let me out of here!"

Jeremy was in bed in his condo on campus. That was weird; he usually woke up back in class. He was so happy it was over that he didn't care.

Classes that day breezed by. He was exhausted, but he had an exam the next day and had been so stressed about fear class that he couldn't study much before. Leaving the library that night, he walked alone across the quad. He suddenly noticed something in the night, in the trees up ahead. His heart stopped racing as he realized it was a sophomore leaning up against one of the trees after what likely was a few too many drinks.

"Need some help getting home?"

The kid shook his head. "Fresh air ... and then some fresh air."

Jeremy nodded. He'd been there. He kept going along his way. It had only been a couple of minutes when he heard the steps behind him.

"You decided to join me after all?" He turned to see the kid, but he wasn't stumbling anymore. Instead, he was standing straight, held up with a knife through his chest. The man holding the knife grinned at Jeremy through the goat mask. Jeremy screamed and ran. He could hear the man behind him. He rounded a corner and ducked into a window well. He waited. For five minutes, he didn't hear or see anything. The window beside him was already open. He backed up into it and started to lower his legs. He heard footsteps again and lowered himself more quickly until he realized the sound was coming from the room he was dropping into. He felt the hand tightly around his leg. He knew the knife was coming, that the pain he had felt so many times before was coming. He was pulled into the room so quickly that his head hit the floor, and it knocked him out.

Jeremy woke up in a sweat in his bed on campus. Something was wrong. Was he trapped in the simulation? He ran to Mr. Moreau's office and banged on the door.

"Office hours are later today!"

"I need to talk to you now!" Jeremy kept banging his hand against the door.

Mr. Moreau opened the door, and Jeremy pushed past him and sat down. "Fear class isn't ending!"

"What do you mean?"

"Fear class. Two days ago. I completed the simulation. I died, but the... the monster came back the next day and attacked me again. I'm trapped somehow."

"Jeremy, we don't have fear class for another two months."

"You're lying!"

Jeremy was irate, banging his hands on the table, but then calmed down as something dawned on him. "This is the problem. Why did I even think you could help me? You are just a function of the computer and I'm trapped in here somehow. You know what, since this won't even matter, you can go to hell."

Moreau was about to scold Jeremy, but he had already left the room and slammed the door. Nick Moreau was angry but thought he might have been more accommodating. He knew Jeremy's past and knew that he had been a bit unstable.

Jeremy remained in Nick's thoughts as he went about the rest of his day, even as he made his way home. He thought about how he should call Jeremy's parents, so they knew to check on him. In fact, he couldn't believe he hadn't done that yet. Nick reached for his phone when a sound startled him. There was a shape on his back porch, and he couldn't believe his eyes. Jeremy stood there silently as if in response to his thoughts. He put the phone down and slowly walked to the door.

"Jeremy?"

Jeremy didn't respond; he simply stared. Nick didn't know what to do. Jeremy made him nervous, but perhaps he could correct his earlier failure and provide him with some guidance. He rested his hand on the back door and then opened it. "Hey buddy, you can't come by like this. It's okay this once, though. Let's chat so that I know you're okay."

Jeremy stepped in, and instead of replying, he quickly brought a pipe to Nick's head.

Nick came to and could feel the blood dripping down his head. He was tied down to a chair in his hallway leading to the front door. Jeremy was pacing back and forth.

"Jeremy, you have to let me out! What are you doing?" Nick could tell that his head was in bad shape. It hurt to even speak.

"Not until you understand."

"Understand what? This is a crime, but we can still be okay if you let me out."

"The one that visits me. He doesn't visit anyone else. I ask the other kids what they see during their fear training, and it is nothing like this, but now you will see, or at the very least feel."

Jeremy slowly drew the knife along Nick's gut as he screamed.

"Jeremy, you are killing me! There is no monster! You are going to kill a man."

“No. He was right behind me on the way over here. I could feel myself being watched all day.”

“There is no such thing! What do you think is happening? That you are in fear class? What if you are in fear class, and the fearful situation being created is just that you got close to killing me?”

Jeremy now seemed uncertain. He kept looking at the door to the house and back at Nick. Nick could barely keep his eyes open now. “Help! Help!” He shouted a couple more times, but he was losing his strength. He thought he could hear someone coming to the door. His eyes finally shut, and he drifted off as he could hear Jeremy yelling, “Look!”

Nick opened his eyes and was sitting in his doctor’s office. “Congratulations, Nick, another year down. You’ve completed your fear exercise for this year.”

Nick got his bearings and wiped the sweat from his forehead. He had never sweated this much before. “Doctor, something is wrong in there, the computer ... it’s evil.”

Noah's Secret

"Books only had one ending." Thomas leaned back. "Can you believe that?"

What was Thomas doing here? Something in my mind called out to me. It was as if I was trying to remember a dream. I looked around the room. The harder I searched for the answer, the more I pushed it away. Eventually, I was in the moment with Thomas. There were no vestiges of my prior concerns.

"What do you mean?"

"It wasn't interactive where you could impact the outcome. You simply were an observer, reading or viewing what was happening. The ending that the author laid out for you was the only ending available. Originally, they were written on paper, then electronically, and then through your uplink. Each one was a distinct genre. They were rigid."

"That's insane." My mind raced with the implications. "What if it was a really sad story, and you wanted to change it?"

"You couldn't. It would simply take you down that set path and show you what happened, like a train on the tracks. It can't change that course. It can slow down, or go back to the start, but the only end is down that path. It doesn't matter if the train goes in a loop, through a dark tunnel, or off a cliff. You can't change course. You're trapped, I guess."

"That's terrifying."

"No. It's exciting. Everything we do now we water down. If we don't like the end of the story, we change it. If we don't want to know what is in a haunted house, we turn the corner. True excitement, true release, comes from relinquishing that control." Thomas was leaning forward in his chair, smiling. It was an old wooden rocking chair. Where were we? No room I knew had a chair like that. I couldn't remember getting here, but part of me knew the room.

"Thomas, what..." I couldn't articulate my thoughts. Again, they faded away.

Thomas looked concerned. "Is something wrong?"

"No, it's just a headache. Sorry, keep talking. How did you find this out?"

"I was researching it. The last book to be written as a set story was called *Noah's Secret*. There is a cult following for the book in the darkest parts of the web. This guy, Noah, apparently created a pirated upload since they wouldn't let him load it."

"It was named after the author? Did he write anything else?"

"Nothing. Complete recluse. He was a writer at the time when everyone was just starting to be connected by uplink. He hated the uplink and felt it was taking away the mystery in the world. There are only a couple quotes from him and this story that no one seems to know much about."

I was starting to feel better. I loved stuff like this, crumbs from the past. With everything in the world cataloged and understood, so few mysteries were left. "What are the quotes?"

"Okay, you'll like this one. He sounds like a complete psycho.

"'Writing is an author choosing to share a secret with you. These secrets need darkness to exist, and the journey is only real if the reader relinquishes control. That is the price the reader must pay to learn the secret. These interactive stories, immersing yourself in these worlds, are exciting, but they abandon the old pact between writer and reader. I will bring this darkness back so that secrets may exist again.'"

"I completely agree with some of what he's saying, but what does he mean by darkness? That gives me no sense about the book. What is the book about?"

"It's a horror story. That's the only description I've been able to find on the entire net. People talk about it as if they have heard of it but never read it. Teenagers will get a tattoo of the title, but they won't know what it means. They just know it's rebellious. No one speaks as if they have read the book. Maybe they have and simply don't talk about it; it's illegal to be found with a copy on your network." Thomas lowered his voice to a whisper. "I got us a copy, though."

I suddenly didn't feel good. That sleeping animal in the back of my brain reared up. "I hate horror stories, you know that. I can barely do them even when in full control. I can't imagine one with an ending someone else picked for me."

"I know, but I also know that no one is as curious as you." Thomas smiled his usual smile. "Think of it as a treasure hunt. This is something that no one else knows. No one else has been on this ride, at least that I've found."

He had me. "Okay, upload it before I change my mind. Let's give it a read."

“Okay. Remember, there is no way out of the story except to go to the end. If it’s long, it’s long. If it’s scary, it’s scary. We have to go to the end.”

I nodded.

“Three, two, one, go.”

I waited and squeezed my eyes shut. Nothing happened. I slowly opened one eye and then the second. I was sitting in a room. Why was I here?

“Thomas…” I couldn’t form the words for my concern. This wasn’t where I was supposed to be. Was it? There was a silent scream in my mind that slowly faded.

Thomas started talking, but it wasn’t in reply to anything I did. “Books only had one ending.” Thomas leaned back. “Can you believe that?” He was sitting in an old wooden rocking chair.

“What do you mean?” I asked.

Scorpio Motors

"This is the newest model we have," the saleswoman said, pointing at the car at the front of the showroom. It was a beautiful silver with a hint of blue.

"Oh, I don't need anything like that." Gillian knew her husband would be angry at her for even looking at the higher-end model.

"Well, before you decide against it, you must know that this meets the highest safety standard ever created. And I mean ever. Across any car. You have children, don't you?"

"Yes."

"Exactly. I'm a parent myself. The safety of our children is everything. With this car, the company established auto driving protocols to definitively favor the owner, even over pedestrians. That is one of a kind, you can't get that preference from other cars."

"What does that mean?"

"Auto driving is a bit of a gray area when it comes to high-risk decisions, and the programming by other companies has always had to strike a bit of a balance. For example, if you can avoid getting hit and killed by another car that runs a light, but it means you must swerve and hit a pedestrian to do it, what does the car do? With other car companies, it is uncertain; sometimes it creates an internal conflict, and the car stops moving, which ironically ensures that the passengers get killed in the accident." The saleswoman then whispered, "Our car here would save your life every time."

"By killing the pedestrian?"

"Yes. An awful thing, I agree. But if you think about your children in the car, it suddenly becomes a lot easier. I would do anything for my kids." She smiled and touched the top of Gillian's arm.

"The government lets you do this?"

"You look like a smart lady, so I'll tell you exactly what's happening. We are in court with a couple of advocacy groups, but this model's sales revenue would let us fight the legal battle for years. It is the number one selling car in the country, the Scorpio 6000. We only have four left for sale at this dealership. Regardless of what you feel about the programming, it is better to have your family in one of these rather than outside one…" The saleswoman managed a small laugh.

"I don't know if I could ever buy a car that values life like that."

"We have been talking here about an extreme hypothetical situation to help explain the default decision-making process. It isn't likely to ever actually occur. I think the thing that would be more relevant, and is the true innovation, is the owner safety default."

"How does that work?"

"When you buy the car, you register as an owner in the programming dashboard. So, you would register as an owner when you purchase it today, and when you get home, you register each of your family members as owners. The car takes a distinct view of owners versus other individuals. Your kids are going to be teenagers soon, and I'm sure there will be lots of times when you aren't around, or when they are driving with friends. You know how it is growing up."

Gillian thought back to when Aidan used to pick her up in the middle of the night after she snuck out of her parents' house. It was always exhilarating, but as she thought about it, she remembered how he had always been casually drinking. She didn't want that for her daughter.

As if in response to her thoughts, the saleswoman continued, "Let's imagine your daughter has a boyfriend who is driving her home one night. As with all kids, he probably wants to show off and turns the auto-driving off. Let's imagine he makes a wrong turn or swerves into traffic. Normal driver response is to protect the driver's side, it's human nature. That would mean putting your daughter in harm's way. The Scorpio 6000 is different because as soon as it senses the collision and confirms that an owner is in the car, it will attempt to avoid the collision completely, but if it can't, it will take control to protect the owner's side of the car."

Gillian didn't know how she felt about all of this. It was something she would never have had to think about only a couple of years ago. "It protects you at all times?"

"Yes, it is the leader in safety."

"Pretty unbelievable technology. If our oven had this programming, I don't think it would let my husband cook his famous meatloaf."

The lady simply stared at Gillian, forcing her to elaborate. "My husband's meatloaf is terrible; some might say a health hazard." The lady nodded.

Gillian was less interested in small talk now. "To be honest, I would need to discuss this with my husband as we didn't consider this car an option. It's a little expensive too. Can I hold one of the models for a couple of days?"

"You seem nice, but my boss wouldn't let me. We will sell these four in the next day or two." The saleswoman must have seen Gillian's face fall. "How about this? You can buy this one, but I'll set you up with a return policy for two days so that you can return it for a full refund if your husband does not like it."

There was a long pause. Gillian thought that Aidan would have to understand the safety features' importance. Perhaps he would even be happy about it. "Okay, let's do it."

Gillian sat in the car and registered herself as an owner. A calm voice welcomed her. "Where would you like to go, Gillian?"

The car drove smoothly, the seats were comfortable, and Gillian felt safe. She knew this was the right choice for her kids. But as she pulled into the driveway, her mood changed, and her stomach turned. Aidan was sitting on the porch having a drink. He had a scowl on his face, meaning he had been in a bad mood after work, and it would have only gotten worse with beer. He lifted himself up off the porch.

"What is that?" he bellowed. "We agreed you were getting the same model we had before." His eyes were like stars under his thick eyebrows and flowing black hair. His forearms were thick, and his shirt was open. He was made for a different time and should have been born a hundred years ago, but here he was. She had found it appealing when she was younger, but that also felt as if it was a different time.

"They will allow us to return it, but I think we will keep it. It is the safest we can get for the kids. It makes several important safety distinctions that..." He twisted her wrist, and he walked her back toward the car.

"Ow, what are you doing?"

"We're taking this back! I don't want to hear it."

She squealed as he threw her in the passenger side of the car. She looked out the window at a neighbor staring blankly. It was a familiar scene.

He got in the driver's seat. "I can't believe you didn't get us the right one. I have to do everything myself. Car, take us back to the dealership... Previous location."

"Sorry, user not recognized."

He slammed his hand against the dash in protest.

"Don't! If we break it, they won't let us take it back. It won't recognize you as an owner until..." Something came over Gillian, and she paused. "Never mind. Drive us there if you want."

"We are talking about this when we get home." Aidan switched to manual control and spun out of the driveway.

Gillian looked out the window in silence as he drove, trying to hide as close to the window as possible. She didn't know if she wanted the drive to be short or long, but it went quickly. As they pulled into the Scorpio dealership, Aidan grabbed her wrist again, tighter than before. He leaned in close with an anger that made the air electric.

"Listen, I can't believe you made me come back here. This is the last—"

Aidan's eyes widened as the car suddenly sped just inside the entrance. "What is this piece of garbage doing? I told you not to get one of these damn cars!" He was slamming his foot on the brake, but nothing happened. The car looped around the parking lot once, then picked up more speed. It turned sharply with a surprising precision for the out-of-control scene. Tires squealing, it headed right for the metal scorpion sculpture in the middle of the parking lot. Aidan clawed at the wheel, but nothing happened. They both screamed as the car jumped the curb and for a second, they were airborne. Time seemed to slow down. Aidan looked Gillian in the eye, and then suddenly, his eyes were different. Gillian realized the car had stopped moving, and she was the only one screaming. The car was perched on the scorpion statue, and the scorpion's tail had impaled Aidan. He wasn't breathing, wasn't squirming; she knew he was dead. She could hear people collecting in the parking lot, but everything felt quiet and slow after the crashing sounds of metal and glass. Suddenly, a voice startled her.

"You have arrived safely at the destination, Gillian. I have called EMS and assessed my repairs. They should only take a week." Gillian looked around her at the car. She brushed her hair out of her face, took a deep breath ... and smiled.

The Importance of Goals

Jason stared out the window, beset by melancholy that only comes at dusk. There was no excitement about things to come and no pride in things accomplished. Doug and Ryan would arrive soon with beers, as always. In his hands, Jason held a silver card. He put it down on the table, started to walk away, and then picked it back up again. It had a weight to it that surprised him. All it said was *Goals* and an address: 657 Eagle Road.

Doug and Ryan let themselves in through the front door, and Jason turned to meet them. They greeted each other with a half-hug, half-wrestling move and then settled down and put the game on. Each of them sat in their usual spots: Doug and Ryan on the couch, Jason in his chair. The three had been friends since elementary school.

Ryan put his feet up and looked at the others. "Should we put money on the game?"

"You never have any money," Jason said.

"Look, I'll even take New York tonight."

"New York is always a winner," Doug said.

Ryan looked at him. "New York lost five in a row."

Jason smirked. "Doug has never let a lack of knowledge prevent him from forming an opinion."

Doug looked at Ryan. "What's that big orange sweater you're wearing anyway?"

The sweater was fading and much too large. Ryan looked down at the sweater and realized he had no defense. "I wanted something that said to everyone I'm not worth mugging. And I must tell you, it worked like a charm. Someone even gave me money. Hell, I probably made more than you today, Doug."

Jason had stopped listening to the banter of the other two. He knew how it went. Doug was probably about to tell Ryan that every one of his photos looked like the ones the news channels would show when he finally committed a crime. Or Ryan was probably telling Doug he was responsible for his love of music because listening to anything was better than listening to Doug. The conversation drifted in and out as Jason flipped the card over in his hand.

A week ago, out for a run past the dam, Jason had stepped past the fence and, for a moment, stood on the edge. The water was shallow after the dry summer, and he knew he'd never survive the fall, but he also knew he wouldn't jump. He stood there anyway, wanting to see how close he could get to a completely different path in life. Being at the edge of that choice between two completely different outcomes was exhilarating. The universe had no idea what was about to happen. He stood there for a second, only a second, because there was so much possibility in the choice, and it had fascinated him.

Jason cleared his throat.

"Guys, are you happy with where we are in life?"

"Is this because Doug and I only got one order of wings the other night when we should have got two? I've been giving that a lot of thought."

"I'm serious. Are you happy with this?"

Neither responded. The three of them were silent; that usually only occurred when there was food.

"Have a beer. That always helps." Ryan reached down, picked up a beer, and tossed it toward Jason.

Jason caught the beer and opened it. "Stupid question, you're right. Best friends and cold beer. I can't imagine what else I'd need."

Doug suddenly spoke up. "It's not stupid." He looked at his friends. "I'm not happy. This is great, but it's not what I wanted. There was a time when I pictured myself in a big house with a family at this age. I wonder what happened. Sometimes, I think it's because I don't want those things, and other times, I wonder if I didn't try hard enough."

Ryan started to look as serious as possible with two open beers in his hands. "I guess you've got a point. I thought I'd be richer by twenty-five. Hell, I'd even take not being poor. I'm still working a job I hate just to make ends meet, but what else will I do?"

"I've been giving it a lot of thought." Jason surveyed the others. "I was out this afternoon and was going to sign up for one of those seminars at the Studio a couple blocks south of us. It was on achieving your dreams."

"Isn't that the place you always joked about joining to pick up girls?" Ryan asked.

"Yeah, but I never went inside. I was standing at the entrance when a man approached me and gave me his business card." Jason handed the card to the others.

"Fancy." Doug held the card in his hands. "He say anything?"

"He said goals are what we tell people we want to get what we're too scared to articulate. If I was looking into these sessions, it meant I had goals that hadn't been achieved. He said I needed real help and that I didn't have the will to make life difficult for myself if I didn't achieve what I wanted. He said he would be holding a spear to my back."

Doug laughed. "Was he more or less pretentious than I'm imagining?"

"Always more."

"But he didn't work at the Studio?"

"No. He thinks he has something more to offer than those seminars."

"Let's do this then!" Ryan stood up.

"We don't have to go. I'm just saying it might be something we want to look at in the future. Worst case, it could be a crazy story, or maybe it could get us some of the things we want."

Doug was slowly putting bottles into a bag. "I'm with Ryan, let's just go. I'll bring beer since having more drinks is a real goal. Look how committed I am."

"Fine, let's do it."

—— «» ——

657 Eagle Road was a four-story low-rise with only a couple of windows on one side, outlining a stairwell. Jason was buzzed from chugging a beer in the cab ride over. It seemed both smart and dumb. Ryan had a bottle of whiskey with him, and he waved at the building. "Is this it?"

Jason looked at the card again. "Yep. I can see it on the buzzer."

Ryan laughed. "It didn't occur to me how weird an eight o'clock evening arrival was until now. They're going to think we're here to rob them or something. I mean, look at my sweater."

The buzzer rang, and a voice answered, "Down the stairwell to basement level three."

“I’m going to bring this,” Ryan said, putting his bottle in his left hand and opening the door with his right. Jason would typically have argued but felt it was good for the people at Goals to see how much help they needed. He followed Ryan through the door and heard Doug’s heavy breathing behind him. The stairwell was narrow and dimly lit. The entrance to basement level three was a black door Ryan was already stepping through.

The inside was so bright and clean that it took their eyes time to adjust. Everything was in stark contrast to the building. It reminded Jason of a lab. Small blue lights outlined the edges of the room. The man who had given Jason the card stood just inside the entrance as if he had always stood there.

“My name is Mr. Gardner. Welcome, please come in.”

Jason wished he had brought his beer instead of drinking it all in the cab.

In the room behind the foyer was a row of five black chairs. Two beautiful women moved small pieces of equipment around behind the chairs. Doug said, “Looks like a themed barbershop. I mean, I like it, but—”

“Don’t you worry, sir; you will see we only use the most advanced technology. That will become more and more apparent. Now, gentlemen, sit, and I’ll tell you how we can help.”

Doug looked tired and was already sitting down. Ryan tossed himself into one of the chairs and sat there with his bottle. Jason slowly sat down.

“Now, you’re all here because you want something and need help getting it. You don’t need books or lessons; you need something that drives you. There’s a part of all of us that can achieve everything we want; Goals simply brings that part to the forefront. It’s the same way a tough situation or a good coach motivates you. All we do is insert something small that causes you pain if you haven’t achieved your goals. Simplicity is beauty, gentlemen. The pain increases as you get closer to the predetermined deadline. It’s cheap, too, when you think that we’re changing your life forever for the better. We plan to expand. Society needs us. One day we’ll just be something everyone does each year, like going to the dentist. We’ll drive humanity forward but need more success stories first; our fees are small until then.” This part seemed to pain Mr. Gardner. Jason thought about how the man probably imagined speaking to executives instead of three idiot friends.

Ryan took a swig of his bottle and passed it to Doug. "Let me get this straight. We pay you to put a little device in us that shocks us if we don't achieve our goals. What if we want to stop participating in this?"

"What you can do, and what sometimes occurs, is pay us to halt the service."

"Why would I do something where the likely outcome is I pay you again on the back end?" Jason was impressed that Ryan was speaking, let alone intelligently.

"I would say this more common outcome is still a successful one. Imagine you set a monetary goal and work exceptionally hard but don't achieve it. You'll still likely be approaching it, or at least significantly richer than you are today. Despite not reaching your goal, you would have more than enough money to pay to remove our technology and have money left over for many of the things you'd originally dreamed of. That sounds like an outcome you'd gladly pay for." Mr. Gardner didn't smile. There was no reassurance. It was as if he already knew the three men had agreed.

"Now, gentlemen, what are your goals, and when do you want them by?"

Jason was shocked to hear Doug speak first. "I want a wife and two kids by the time I'm twenty-nine. She needs to be smart, beautiful, and driven."

"I will let you evaluate those more qualitative aspects. Wife and two kids it is." Mr. Gardner whispered something to one of the assistants.

Ryan shouted his. "I want a million dollars by the age of thirty." He passed the bottle of whiskey to Jason. "Come on, buddy. What do you want? You're the one we must thank for bringing us."

Jason could feel one of the ladies already doing something on his neck. It felt like a small tattoo, but only for a second. He wasn't focused on that, though. Despite all his problems, he suddenly couldn't form them into a legitimate goal. He took a big swig from the whiskey bottle to help him think. Ryan gave him the thumbs up, which was returned with another bottle salute.

"Okay, I also want a million dollars by thirty for my first goal. We can all celebrate that together."

"Sir, I usually stress that people do not pick multiple goals. They can find it extremely challenging."

Jason took another swig of whiskey. "You trying to hold me back? Trying to keep all the success for yourself?"

Mr. Gardner smiled slightly and shook his head. "What is your second goal, then?"

"I want to outlive both these idiots."

"Done. That's an interesting one."

"Okay, gentlemen. I look forward to watching your progress over the years. I feel these goals will make you known to the world, and in turn, they will also help me achieve my goals. Congratulations."

A couple of high fives and handshakes followed; Mr. Gardner didn't participate in the high fives. Ryan invited him to the club afterward but said he had work to do. The three friends partied for most of the night, already celebrating what they believed to be their imminent success.

—— «» ——

Jason woke up and saw the missed calls on his phone. The first call was from Doug, and the second number Jason didn't recognize. Doug had moved a few hours south for work two years ago and routinely called after several drinks to shout that he missed them. Jason played the voicemail.

"Jason, it's Doug. The pain. It won't stop. It's everything now." His breathing was labored, and Jason couldn't make out large parts of the message. "I'm driving to your house. I need to talk to you ... about everything you remember from that night. Remember that night? Goals. Almost four years ago now. I can't find any record. It's as if ... it can't be, but my god, the pain, it's real. We must stop this." There was a scream, and the message ended.

Jason went to play the second voicemail. He was horrified that he already knew what it was. "Mr. Jason Seal. I'm sorry to call you at this hour, but you're listed as Doug Barnes's emergency contact. There's been an accident. Please call Mountain View Hospital as soon as possible."

Jason immediately called Ryan.

"Ryan, it's Jason. Something happened to Doug. I think he worked himself up and got in an accident. I don't know — I don't know if he made it. I called you first."

"Was it the pain?" Ryan sounded surprisingly calm.

"What?"

"Never mind. Let's talk in person."

Jason and Ryan headed to the hospital together. In the car, Ryan asked Jason to play the message twice, but that was all. Neither of them knew what to say yet, so they simply waited to speak with the doctor.

"He suffered a stroke, and his car veered off the road. We couldn't save him. I'm sorry."

Ryan seemed more focused than sad. "What was the time of death?"

"Around seven a.m. We brought him here, but there was nothing we could do. Again, I'm so sorry." The doctor slowly walked away and appeared to be as shocked as they were.

Ryan got his phone out. "I have to make a call."

Jason looked at him. "What?"

He held up his hand as the phone was already ringing. "Hello, Ms. Barnes. I'm so sorry. Yes, we came to the hospital when we heard about it but didn't make it in time. When do you land today? We'll see you then. I have one question for you. The doctors need to know what time he was born... Yes, it's a weird question. I don't know why. Okay, seven in the morning, I'll tell them. Safe flight."

Ryan turned to Jason. "Seven in the morning, Jason! That's exactly when he turned twenty-nine. Goals killed him because he didn't achieve what he wanted."

"That can't be true. That entire place was just smoke and mirrors to get you thinking positively. Doug was going crazy near the end. He said there were voices in his head. Come on! Voices in his head. That isn't how a normal person talks. He stressed himself out to the point it caused a stroke."

Ryan looked calmly at Jason with sympathy, which was rare for him. His voice was soft as he spoke. "Have you started to get the headaches?"

Jason looked away from Ryan. "I've always had migraines since I was a kid. They get bad this time of year."

"They aren't migraines. You know the ones I'm talking about. The steady pain. It starts at the base of your neck and creeps into your head. At first, it was so small that I could forget it was there, but now it's my constant companion."

Jason knew that Ryan could see the pain behind his eyes. "I went to the doctor a couple of months ago to ask him about the migraines. He said there was no cause. Painkillers are getting to the point where they no longer have an impact. As weird as it is, though, today I feel better. Maybe it can get better?"

"It only gets worse. We both know that. We've seen that with Doug! You're probably only feeling better because there's so much adrenaline running through you from everything today."

"You're probably right." Jason sat down on the floor with his back against the wall. "What do we do?"

"I don't know. What if we went public? Told everyone."

"No one would believe us. I don't even believe myself when I say it. What would we even say? I need a million dollars because my life depends on it?" Jason was a child again as tears started to stream down his face.

"I don't know what we'll do. We'll figure it out, though. At least we know, and we have a bit of time. Doug didn't have that knowledge." Ryan sat down beside Jason. "Jason, how much money do you have?"

"A hundred and thirty thousand. You?"

"About a hundred. I could sell my car for twenty."

"We have a little over a year until your birthday, Ryan. Mine's shortly after."

"I know! We need a solution before the pain becomes debilitating." They were silent as they remembered Doug's screams. "Okay, we invest it."

"We don't know anything about investing. If we lose the money, all we've done is seal our fates."

"Think about Mr. Colt. He lives in that massive house down the road. He made all that money on the stock of his company."

"We put it all in his stock?"

"That thing tripled in the past year. You have a better idea?"

"No... I guess it's as good an idea as any." They both sighed.

—— «» ——

Jason banged on the door of Ryan's apartment. "Ryan! Have you seen it? You did it!"

Ryan opened the door and embraced Jason. "Can you believe it? It's more than doubled!"

They looked at the stock price on their phones, and for a moment, they forgot the pain.

"What if we just get to be rich? For the last five months, I've been unable to see a way out of this that doesn't end in death or darkness. What if we just get to live now?"

They laughed. But it was a short reprieve; after that day, the stock slowed its advance and then started to tick down.

Two weeks later, they sat on the couch at Ryan's.

"Jason, we have a little over half a million now. The stock keeps dropping. We need to do something."

"I know. The pain keeps coming back stronger every day. It's crushing me. I don't know what to do."

"Maybe we go to the casino and put it all on black. What other option do we have? We are down to three weeks. The stock isn't going to get there in time, and it looks like it might do the exact opposite. Putting it all on black, any idiot can do that and win twice. We could be that idiot. I've seen it happen five times in a row for a guy."

Jason was tired and simply nodded. He didn't believe in the plan. The only thing he did believe was that he was dying. He tried to give Ryan a small smile. "Hey Ryan, thanks for always looking for a way out of this. Thank you for fighting for us."

"Of course, buddy. We got into this together, and we'll get out together."

Ryan and Jason walked into the casino. The two of them were covered in sweat and constantly rubbing their temples; they were at a point where pain medication provided no solace. Despite this, they did not stand out in the crowd. The closest major casino had a table maximum of $250,000. This was certainly not a major casino, and the bet was unlimited here. The higher stakes came with a rougher crowd and fewer bright lights. Ryan and Jason had the same crazy eyes as the other patrons; everyone was trying to escape something.

The day before, Ryan and Jason had decided they'd put it all on black; they couldn't handle the stress of determining at the table. The two of them handed their cash through the bars and waited for their chips; the total chip count was

$514,000. Two men in suits came to double-check the count and then passed the chips to Ryan.

Ryan made room for himself at the side of the roulette table, put the money down on black, and stepped back. Based on peoples' reactions, there was rarely a bet that came close. A man was called over to watch. Jason wondered if people knew they were playing for their lives. Looking around, he guessed that wasn't uncommon.

The pit boss nodded at the table, and the dealer spun the roulette ball.

"I can't watch." Ryan stepped back from the table, and Jason stepped in to fill his place. Jason had already assumed they'd lost and had no problem watching. He'd given up hope, so watching the ball bounce back and forth was no stress. The ball slowed down, bounced twice, and landed.

"Black seventeen."

The dealer paid out their winnings; over half a million. Jason gathered the chips in his hands, and the pain suddenly retreated. A peace came over him, and he didn't move. A terrible thought had formed in his brain, which was now complete; it would remain his companion. He stood there with all the peace and health everyone took for granted.

Ryan nudged him on the back. "We have to get two million, so we have a million each. One more time."

Ryan guided Jason's hands, and he slowly put the chips on black again. The pain crept back. Jason and Ryan watched as the roulette ball bounced around the wheel. The pain in Jason's head started to gain momentum. He now knew what was evident to whatever was inside him; the pain returned entirely as the ball landed on red. Their money was gone. All Jason was left with was the thought in the back of his head.

Ryan looked at Jason. Neither spoke. Ryan looked like he was about to say something but then leaned to the side and threw up, partially from pain and partially from shock. Two security guards asked them to leave, and they headed to the street. The two of them sat on the curb.

Jason banged his hands on his head. "I can barely think it hurts so much!"

Ryan wiped his mouth and looked at him. "I've got a couple of guns in my apartment."

"What would you have me do? Kill myself?"

Ryan was quiet. "No. We rob someone."

"We aren't those kinds of people."

"There's no kind of person! Only certain kinds of situations! Do you want to die?"

Jason sat there, thinking. The pain had increased even in the time they'd been talking. Sweat was dripping down his face. He came to terms with the fact that very soon, he'd either have to point a gun at himself or someone else.

He said one word. "Who?"

"Mr. Colt, he has more money than he needs. Think about how much he made on his shares this past year. He doesn't need it. We need it. We go into his house, put a gun to his head, and tell him to transfer us the money, or we kill him." Jason didn't respond, but Ryan knew he had him. "We go tomorrow. If it doesn't work, we try something else the following day. Come on. Let's walk to my place and get some sleep."

Jason lay awake on Ryan's couch. It was a studio apartment, and Ryan lay in the bed a few feet away. As Jason looked at the ceiling, he called out to Ryan, "It's a little peaceful."

"Of course. It's nighttime."

"No. I mean, having only one problem to solve is almost peaceful. Before all this, I worried about what people thought of me, how I was doing at work, and what I would do on weekends. Tonight, lying here, I'm only focused on one thing. Unfortunately, one thing happens to be surviving, but all the same, it's peaceful only to have one thing. Nothing else matters."

Ryan didn't reply. Jason knew he was doing the same thing: thinking and looking into the darkness. They tried to sleep.

Ryan and Jason stood over the table the following evening, organizing their masks and guns.

"Are you sure it doesn't make more sense to rob someone who lives farther away?"

"That's the beauty of it. No one would ever suspect someone in the same neighborhood. When the police respond, we'll simply be walking around the neighborhood. It's our neighborhood! We were at his house a few months back for that community party. Our fingerprints have a reason to be there, not that they'd ever find any."

"I'm just a little nervous that our main defense is that this is too stupid for anyone to do."

"I honestly can't think of anything else, so maybe we are stupid enough for this." Ryan picked up his gun and handed one to Jason. "Come on. We should go." Jason looked at the gun as Ryan turned his back and opened the door for them to leave.

Ryan and Jason crept through the night to Mr. Colt's house. The house was large and set in the back of the lot.

Ryan's breathing was heavy. "I think I'm more nervous than you, Jason. I thought you'd have chickened out after all the convincing it took."

Jason grimaced. "I've come to terms with where we're at and what we need to do. What I need to do."

"Okay. That's good. I don't see any lights. Mr. Colt should be asleep."

They kept close to the ground and slinked to the back of the house. The basement door was open, with only the screen door pulled across. Ryan expected the alarm system couldn't be armed with one of the doors still open. He pulled out his knife and cut the screen. He stepped through the hole, and Jason followed.

Ryan went slowly, step by step, through the basement and up the stairs. He was taking his time, letting his eyes adjust to the dark. Jason followed. On the main floor, they walked to the back hall leading to Mr. Colt's room. Every step was exhilarating in a way neither of them had expected. They walked into the bedroom. The openness of it felt weird. There was no door, simply a hallway, and then they rounded the corner to see him asleep in bed. Jason didn't know what to do, but Ryan acted immediately.

"Get up!"

Mr. Colt reared up and screamed.

"Shut up, or I shoot. I need you to hear what I'm saying."

Mr. Colt stopped screaming. With shaking hands, he reached for his glasses on the bedside table. He brought them to his face.

"I'm listening." His voice trembled.

"I'm going to give you an account number. You then transfer two million dollars to the account, or we'll kill you."

"You're going to kill me over two million dollars?"

"Yes!" Ryan stepped toward the bed, raised his hand, and brought the gun down on Mr. Colt's head. The man crumpled. Ryan pulled him out of the bed and threw him to the floor. He raised his boot and stepped down. Jason grabbed Ryan and pulled him back.

"He knows you're serious."

Ryan looked down and could barely make out Mr. Colt's face beneath the blood. He realized he'd gone too far but couldn't say anything.

"I'll... transfer... the money." Mr. Colt's breathing was labored.

"Put your guns down!"

Ryan was trying to understand how such strong words had come from the man who lay crumpled before them. He heard it again. "Put your guns down now!" A police officer was standing in the hallway behind them, and they could see a flashlight in the yard outside.

The pain was returning. Ryan looked at Jason and started to lower his gun. He couldn't see Jason's eyes beneath the mask, but his mouth shook; he assumed he was starting to cry. Ryan knew it was more than the pain that Jason felt. "It's over, Jason. We aren't going to get the money." Jason's mouth kept shaking, but he still firmly held his gun.

The officer shouted again. "We will not ask again! Put the gun down!"

Ryan looked in shock as Jason still hadn't lowered his gun. "Jason, buddy, you need to put the gun down. There's nothing left for us to do here today."

"I'm sorry, Ryan. I'm so sorry. I got us into this. I wanted a better life for all of us. It was me who sent us to Goals. I killed Doug, and I ... and I'm so sorry for tonight."

"There's nothing to be sorry for. I pushed us to come tonight. Just put the gun down so we can get out of here alive, and we'll figure something else out. Let them come in here and help Mr. Colt. I'm the one who messed up tonight, you just need to put the gun down."

Jason didn't seem to register what Ryan or the officers were saying.

"I can't handle this pain anymore. I'm so sorry. I need your help... your help in achieving my goal."

"Of course, I'll help..."

Jason turned the gun at Ryan and fired. The shot was followed by a second as the officers shot Jason in the arm; he dropped the gun.

As Ryan lay there, as he felt the life draining from his body, he remembered what Jason had joked about many years ago: *I want to outlive both these idiots.*

Amidst the officers shouting, Jason heard a female voice, as if he had earphones: "Congratulations. You've completed one of your goals. You should be very proud." As the police handcuffed Jason, he truly felt good.

Boot Camp

"We paid a million dollars, and the results are better than expected. This is just like you to still not be happy."

Harry put his hands to his face. "It's not that. I'm happy. He just isn't like he used to be. Doesn't he seem different?"

Margot stormed around the bedroom. "Isn't that the point? You hated who he used to be! You were the one that wanted him sent there."

"I wanted Trevor to get better and learn some manners. I wanted someone I could be proud of when people came to the house. I didn't want a different kid."

"Kids change all the time growing up! Trevor was away for an entire month. Of course, he changed during that time. I'm not getting dragged into your world where you are never satisfied. I'm going to sleep." Margot pulled the sheets in a huff and turned the lights off.

Harry lay there, with eyes closed but mind wide open. Eventually, he went downstairs to grab a glass of milk. Sitting in the dark, he pulled out his phone and flipped through old videos. He watched as his boy rode a little bicycle in their backyard. It was a typical family video until Trevor fell, cried for a moment, and then became uncontrollably furious at the bike for hurting him. Trevor kicked the toy multiple times, and Harry laughed while watching the little fists and feet move with such fury amid a string of profanity that seemed as if it couldn't possibly come from such a tiny human. It sounded like an adult had dubbed the video with shocking language interwoven with insults that only a child could think of. Harry chuckled as he heard one insult launched at the inanimate bike over and over: "fart-loving trash pile." A sound out of the dark made him jump, and he looked up from his phone.

"Good evening, Father."

His son was standing only a foot from him in the dark.

"You scared me, buddy. I'm watching old videos. Want to join? We don't have to tell Mom. It can be our secret, like the good old days."

"I'm good, thank you. I need to get back to sleep. I heard the noise and wanted to make sure nothing was wrong."

"You don't have to worry about stuff like that, buddy. Your parents can worry about that."

"Right. Good night, Father."

"Hey, buddy?"

His son turned back and looked at him. "Did anyone hurt you over there? Or did something happen?"

"Everything is great. The institute was exactly what I needed. Good night."

Trevor turned and slowly walked back upstairs to his bedroom. Harry kept his eyes on him as he left. Back in the bedroom, Harry felt a weird desire to lock their bedroom door, but he quickly shook the thought out of his mind. He fell in and out of sleep with his eyes on the open door.

Margot woke up earlier than usual to hear Harry getting dressed.

"It's Sunday, baby. What are you doing?"

"Something blew up at work. I'm going to be tied up for a few days. Sorry, love." Harry grabbed his keys and kissed Margot goodbye.

Harry had never seen his destination personally, so he gave the coordinates to the car: "Solaris Institute, please." The drive took him north, with the ocean to his right and old dark forests to his left. He started drifting off as he relaxed; the car was making good time, and he felt better than last night. He always felt better taking action, even now when he had no idea what to do next.

He didn't wake until hours later when the car's speed noticeably shifted. His eyes opened in time to see the gates, and a sign for the Solaris Institute disappeared behind him. The car drove along a winding road toward another old stone wall and a modern, gated registration house. Two security guards stepped to the door, and the car window rolled down.

"Gentlemen, I'm Harry Benoit. My son was staying with you for a short while. I assume those guns are the reason he is so well-behaved now." Harry pointed at the holster on one of their hips.

The guard didn't laugh but moved the holster slightly so it was less prominent. "We have a lot of wealthy families that trust us with their kids. This is a precaution to deter any would-be kidnappers."

"Of course, of course. So, the reason I'm here is kind of silly. My son thinks he left his hat here, and I promised him I would at least look. I know you taught the kids how important promises are, so I must hold up my end of the bargain." The guards simply looked at him; there was no indication of whether he would be allowed to proceed. "Can I maybe just see the headmaster to tell my son I asked? Or maybe get a note from him that they are looking for it?" The guard whispered something into an earpiece, and the gate behind the registration house opened slowly.

"Thank you."

Harry grabbed the wheel for the first time on the entire trip and slowly drove the car up to the main building. He trusted automatic cars, but maybe less around children. He parked the car in front of the main building and walked up the stairs. A man standing at the top of the stairs nodded and asked him to follow. Once inside, it took Harry's eyes a second to adjust after the bright summer day. Rounding a corner, the man pointed to a chair. "Wait here, please. He will see you soon."

Harry stood beside the chair and began to pace. He was hoping a kid would walk by so he could ask questions, but no one passed. He couldn't remember seeing a single kid even on the grounds. There was almost no movement, to the point that the opening of the door behind him was startling.

A man in a black shirt and stiff gray pants opened the door. "He will see you now. Please follow me." The man carried himself with a stiffness that reminded Harry of the ex-army dads he had grown up around as a kid. He was led through a second door into a larger room with multiple screens on the left. Despite the screens, the room felt like an old-world office with rich wood and an ornate bookshelf. Harry surveyed the volumes as he passed, and his eyes fell on the school's crest with some pompous Latin saying, *Igne Natura Renovatur Integra*, that he guessed simply said, "This will make parents pay twice as much."

The headmaster, Dr. Connor, was a tall man with light brown hair that he had carefully slicked back. His glasses were thin and round, and now that Harry saw him, he couldn't imagine how he could have pictured anyone else in the role. Dr. Connor smiled with very thin lips and proceeded to speak. "Mr. Benoit, you are looking for a hat?"

"I must admit, I'm not here for the hat. I wanted an excuse to see the facility."

Dr. Connor nodded and took his glasses off. "We get that sometimes. What are you curious about?"

"Well, the improvements in our son are so extraordinary that... I've been thinking about making a large donation. I wanted to get a sense of the place under the guise of something else before I got your hopes up. As you know from my work, I am a thorough man, and, despite your amazing job with Trevor, I would need to see the facility before making a donation of this size."

Dr. Connor quickly changed his tone. "Well, this is great news, and we welcome it. We would love to give you a tour. Sheila, please come into my office."

A slender brunette in a lab coat entered the office. The speed at which she arrived implied that, in some capacity, she must have simply been waiting. "Sheila will give you a full tour. I apologize if I seemed cold earlier. Our practices have been attacked before, and we... well, we are very careful now. Enjoy the tour. I will connect with you when you are done and have lunch prepared for us on the grounds. They are spectacular, and I think it impacts the children. It is so difficult to find true nature these days." Trevor hadn't mentioned the grounds even once, but Harry nodded.

"Thank you for everything you have done for my family." Harry departed the office and followed Sheila's lead out the door and down the hallway. The two took a right-hand turn and descended an impossibly long hallway. Harry realized that they must be underground now, with the facility extending into the hillside.

Sheila stopped and pointed to her right. "Here, you can see some of the rooms." Harry stepped through a small door, entering a room a few meters wide and exceptionally sparse. A small desk on one side was beautifully carved out of light wood and stood in contrast with the modern room. To the left of the door, a set of stairs led to a loft with a gray bed set only slightly above the floor. In the loft, ground-level windows looked out into the expansive grounds. Harry realized it was almost like a miniature A-frame cottage if it weren't halfway underground and if there were any way to open the windows.

"We take a very minimalistic approach with the children's quarters. If you remove the noise and interference in a person's life, they eventually realize they are solely responsible for their happiness. We give them the time and space to figure that out. Once they realize that, they also understand that their anger and frustration are fully within their control. It is just easier to start with happiness." She smiled.

Forgetting the gnawing in his mind, Harry suddenly became conversational. "That has a lot of stoic philosophy behind it. It's smart. *Meditations* was my favorite book as a child. I always wanted Trevor to read it, to maybe help him, but I guess he had to live it. No bed of rock, though?"

Sheila smiled; she was attractive. "We will consider your suggestion. Follow me; the meditation studio is next."

The meditation studio was beautiful, an interior room, but the ceiling was exceptionally tall and ended in a skylight that covered the ceiling. The far wall was a thin waterfall, creating an effect that mirrored a white noise machine Harry had at home.

"Meditation is a very important part of our approach. A lot of angry children just aren't comfortable with themselves. A lot of angry adults simply aren't comfortable with themselves. Meditation forces the individual to spend significant periods alone in their heads. They start to understand who they are, and they start to get comfortable with it."

"What if they don't?" Harry said.

"They all do, eventually. Do you know where the most religious group of individuals in the U.S. resides, Mr. Benoit? Where you can ask someone if they believe in God and get a yes nine times out of ten, regardless of race or socioeconomic background?"

"I have no idea. Montana?"

"Death row. Everyone finds peace eventually, in some form or another. It just takes some people a little more time."

Harry looked around the studio. It indeed was beautiful. He just couldn't picture Trevor lying down for meditation. He knew Trevor wouldn't.

"How do you get children to do this? What are the rewards or punishments? Are there physical deterrents?"

"If you are trying to ask if we ever physically touched your son, we did not. We are trying to teach norms for behavior. Our behavior has to be better than the outside world, certainly not worse."

"Of course. Can I see the students? It is difficult to understand everything with just empty rooms."

She shook her head. "It is important that you don't interact with the kids. If a child sees you, they will assume you are a parent coming to get a child before they have completed the program. The kids must understand that the only way through the program is by fully accepting it and coming out the other side."

Harry had to nod, admitting to himself that the explanation made sense.

He pretended to check his watch in a panic. "Look at the time, I have to take a work call." She smiled but stayed exactly where she was. "A little privacy, please!" Harry's anger was uncharacteristic, but she didn't know that. She apologized and retreated around the corner. As soon as she was out of sight, Harry sprinted down a new hallway opposite where they had entered. The hall was long, and he took a left turn and then a right and stopped his sprint to look normal. He figured he had put at least a couple of minutes between them.

There were no signs in any of the hallways. It reminded Harry of a casino where they might not want people to find their way out. He caught his breath and started opening doors, searching for a classroom. It was mainly storage rooms until the third room. The lights took a while to come on, and then it looked distinctly like a dentist's office, except the chair was small, and clamps were attached to the ends to bind feet and wrists. He couldn't believe that Sheila had smugly spoken to him about innovative practices. This was what had changed his son. He started running back to his car.

In his frantic anger, he couldn't remember if he had gone the right way. The place was a maze to him. He checked his phone to call Margot and tell her. There was no signal. Harry heard footsteps around the corner and froze. He stepped back against the wall and poked his head out, seeing a lone man in a gray uniform approaching. He was short and bald. Harry waited until the footsteps were around the corner, then stepped out and pushed the man against the wall.

"Did you hurt my boy?" The man was sputtering, and Harry could feel his heart pounding. Harry suddenly worried he might have given him a heart attack as the man continued to sputter in panic. Harry pulled his arms away and helped prop the man up. "I'm sorry I startled you. I just need some answers. It looks like someone here hurt my son, and I need to know who it was and what happened."

"You're a p-parent of one of our boys?"

"Yes."

The man gave a weak smile. "I understand you must be on edge, having been apart from your son for so long. It's a difficult trial for both parties. That's why visits like this will be great for both of you. It's a treat to finally get a parent that visits, even in light of your firm handshake... I think it's important for the kids to have visitors, and I have told the headmaster many times. Parents need to visit to help validate the progress our students are making. Oh, this is just great."

Harry was taken aback by the man's increasing enthusiasm, especially given their meeting. "Are you a teacher here?"

"Yes, I'm head of the reform program. Neil Childs, pleased to meet you. I know, great last name. I joke with my friends that I didn't need to submit a resume to work here." Neil smiled at him.

"As a teacher here, can you explain how your team uses that chair with the straps? I've seen a lot of things in this world, but I've only seen one reason for a chair like that."

Neil looked puzzled. "Chair?"

"Yes, the chair with the straps on the arms and the legs?"

"Gosh, we don't have any such thing. I'm sorry." Neil's apology seemed to be in fear that Harry's arm would again go against his neck.

Harry grabbed Neil. "It's right back here. Come with me." He half-dragged, half-walked with the man as they rounded two corners. Harry triumphantly threw open the second door on his left to what was a utility closet. The two men both had their mouths wide open.

"Maybe it was this one."

He backtracked and opened the first door down the hallway. It was a server room. Harry slammed his hand against the wall. "This place is a damn maze. I must have gotten turned around. The point is, I saw a chair, a small chair, what you would expect for children, with straps on the arms and legs to hold them down. Is that how you discipline the boys? My boy?" Saying it out loud made Harry feel sick.

"We would never treat a child like that. Come ask them yourself right now." Neil was adamant.

Harry didn't understand if this was some trick but nodded in agreement and followed Neil as he bumbled down the hall. After a few minutes, they opened a door to an indoor green space. Harry saw two more men and women in gray uniforms and eight children amicably playing. One of the men in uniform whispered something to his colleague.

Neil called out to the class. "Matthew, I want you to meet someone."

A boy much taller than the others stood up and came toward the two of them, extending his hand. "My name is Matthew. It is a pleasure to meet you. Are you a new teacher here?"

"I'm a parent."

"Oh, that is lovely." The boy seemed noticeably deflated at the word parent. "Well, it was nice to meet you, but I should return to my game. I'm losing, and they will think I'm hiding from my fate." Matthew smiled and took his seat with the other children. Harry felt a tinge of sadness for how hard the kid tried to be nice. There was desperation to it.

As Harry watched Matthew play, he had a nagging feeling that he recognized him. In the back of his mind, he knew him from somewhere.

"Matthew has made exceptional progress." Neil smiled as he spoke, but it was slightly sad. "He is our longest case. He has been here for five years, and I think he is ready to go home, but the headmaster won't let me graduate him. The headmaster is exceptionally thorough, but, at some point, we will do more harm than good by keeping the kids here. I first recommended Matthew as a graduate of the program two years ago. The headmaster says he will let me know as soon as he believes Matthew is ready, but I worry he will just bring someone else in to head this program who is more aligned with his precise notions. The only thing he and I agree on is that reforming children is one of the greatest callings; you can reduce crime, unhappiness, and domestic abuse, all before it ever happens. I've given everything to this, and maybe I become too attached to the kids, but I don't see why the headmaster and the Executive Committee view that as such a bad thing. Matthew has been here for five years now. It's time he goes home. Five years, and his parents didn't visit once. Can you believe that?"

Harry suddenly remembered where he had recognized the boy. He had seen a promotional package for the institute with Matthew and his parents. Was that right? Margot had shown him the video, and he had just glimpsed it briefly between files for work, but he could have sworn that was him. The parents kept going on about how he seemed like a different boy. Did he say five years?

"How foolish of me." Neil interrupted his thoughts. "Here you are visiting, and I just took you to a random class, not even asking who your son is." Neil brought a tablet out of his pocket. "I have the schedule right here of all the students. What is your last name?"

"It's Benoit, but my boy..." Harry trailed off as Neil pulled up a photo of Trevor on his tablet.

"Looks just like his old man," Neil proclaimed. "Didn't even need the last name."

Harry was suddenly sweating. He rechecked his phone for a signal, but there wasn't any.

"It's just the next classroom. No need to be nervous. This will be great for the two of you to see each other. It won't impact his development at all."

Harry simply nodded. His mouth was dry. Neil led him to a second classroom where four boys worked on a project at a table.

"Trevor, I have a guest for you." Rubbing his neck, Neil added, "He has some of your energy."

With shock, excitement, and terror, Harry met eyes with his son. The same son he had seen in his kitchen the night before. Like a lightning bolt, Trevor exited the table and ran to his dad. He slammed into Harry for a hug, almost knocking him over.

His arms were tight around Harry's neck. Trevor whispered in Harry's ear, "Get me out of this damn place, we won't tell Mom I didn't pass." Harry laughed amidst tears as he held his son tightly.

"You bet, champ," Harry whispered. "Give me a second." Harry turned to Neil with a sudden urgency. "Does that phone of yours work down here? Trevor and his mom need to chat briefly."

Neil smiled. "Certainly. I have a booster in here to make sure I get a signal. Go ahead. Feel free to enter the hall so you two have some privacy."

Harry and Trevor closed the door to the classroom just as a red light and alarm started to go in the hallways. Harry realized this must be for him. He saw a call for Neil on the phone from "office." Harry shoved his back against the door they had come from, to prevent it from opening, and tossed the phone to Trevor. He could feel a push from the door behind him.

"Call your mom's cell right now!"

Trevor looked confused but quickly dialed.

"Dad, she isn't answering. What's going on? I just want to go home."

"Call the house!"

Trevor dialed the house and heard the phone ringing. He recognized the voice that answered, but it wasn't his mother.

"Hello. You have reached the Benoit residence, and this is Trevor Benoit speaking. How may I help you?"

Harry was able to make out the voice on the other end of the phone and felt terrified for his family, but his thoughts were interrupted by his son shouting, "If you touched any of my damn toys, you are dead."

Despite the circumstances, Harry had to smile at hearing his son, his real son, again. "Let's get the hell out of here."

The Icarus

"That concludes our normal lesson for today. As discussed, the second part of the class will be a question-and-answer session. The caliber of the people in this room has afforded us a rare opportunity; I've received permission from the chancellor to discuss the previously forbidden topics of transition and the Icarus. These are words you've previously only whispered late at night between friends. You represent the most curious minds in the world, so I do not doubt that amongst this group, you have pursued these rumors to the point that whisper and conjecture will no longer suffice. Those remaining questions you have always held so dear can be shared today, but I must stress that what we discuss can never be repeated. Hopefully, this open discussion will inspire you for your final paper on what it means to be human." The beautifully wood-paneled classroom was packed. Sitting in theater-style rows six deep, the students nodded in silent agreement at their professor.

Dr. Connor was lying to the students. He hadn't received permission to discuss these topics and never would. He hadn't even asked; he knew that asking would be enough of a crime. As he approached the end of his life, though, the rules seemed less critical. He folded his hands across his chest and winked at the class. His grin highlighted the friendly wrinkles on his face. "Shall we begin?" The students' hands shot up for the rare chance to openly discuss these things.

"Sarah, we'll start with you." Dr. Connor pointed at Sarah's hand as she strained to hold it up as high as she could, her round face alight with excitement. She was one of his brightest.

"Could you please tell us what it was like to be physically alive?"

Dr. Connor surveyed the class from the front of the room. "Let me remind you that if anyone feels uneasy about this question, you should leave immediately." No one moved. Dr. Connor waited a bit longer and then proceeded to address Sarah. "That's a question I expected, but it's not the most interesting. I thought that was the defining question when I was younger, but my views have changed." He paused to lick his lips.

"When I was a young boy, I remember standing in line to be loaded onto the Icarus. At that moment, I tried to treasure the gifts of touch and smell. Bending down, I grabbed a handful of dirt and watched it fall through my fingers. I licked it next and still remember the taste of salt and chalk. I tried to remember everything in case that memory was the only example of living I had after the transition. When I came out the other side, I was surprised I could still feel. Everything remained as real as it had ever been. Looking back, I don't know why I thought it would be different. It's our minds that have always defined our experiences. Nothing has ever existed for us beyond what our mind interprets, and this holds now as strongly as it did before Icarus. If anything, our mind likely presents us with a clearer view of the world now. We have removed any historical obfuscation from inconsistencies in our physical senses. There are only a few of us left that were alive before the transition, and I assure you, none of us noticed a difference. Being alive back then felt exactly as it does now. I need you all to understand that and accept it. It's very important for your mental health that you do not perceive your current state as anything other than alive."

"Thank you. I have one more question, please."

"In the interest of fairness, let's wait to see if we have time for your second question at the end." Sarah's eager face could not hide her disappointment. Dr. Connor walked to the other side of the room and pointed at a young man named Sean.

"Thank you. I apologize because my question is less about psychology. This is such a rare opportunity, though, that I must ask. What was Earth like at the end? We never see it in any of the media or literature."

"Earth was toxic," sighed Dr. Connor. "The Earth we live on now would be as my grandparents knew it, but it's entirely different than the Earth we escaped from. In the last few years, the air has grown poisonous. Severe storms, lasting for weeks and months, swept across the ever-expanding deserts as weather patterns broke down. Certain cities erected domes to protect themselves from an increasingly hostile planet, but even that couldn't last. Most of the world had neither the infrastructure nor resources to protect themselves. There were lines of people outside the dome cities, but they couldn't take everyone. People waited as the winds, the heat, and the toxic air ate away their bodies. Outside the remaining safe zones were makeshift camps as far as the eye could see. That's when the solution of the Icarus was proposed. Who we are as individuals has always been defined by our brains, so there was no reason to leave ten billion people to die simply because of their physical bodies. With this solution, mankind redeemed itself. My last memories on Earth are thankfully of my father helping people make the transition, and not simply of death and decay. That period is rarely mentioned because there's no need to dwell on the darkness that preceded Icarus. We'll leave it at that." Dr. Connor looked away and headed to his desk to drink water. "Okay, I'd like to ask Laura in the back for the next question." Several students' hands had gone down now.

Laura stood up so that everyone could hear. "Did you ever see the Icarus before you transitioned?"

"Again, this isn't the psychological discussion I sought, but I'll answer your question. I did see the Icarus. It's beautiful. My father was involved in the final brain-mapping steps that allowed everyone to be uploaded. As a family, we spent our last moments in a small camp, a thousand feet below the surface, right next to the Icarus site. The Icarus is magnificent, a shiny black box almost the size of a football stadium. It's suspended between a revolving series of super-cooled magnets. Processing all this information means the Icarus runs extremely hot. The air surrounding it is continuously circulated and cooled to prevent overheating. It's amazing to stare at it and understand billions of individuals are contained within."

"I have a question," shouted Keith from the middle of the room.

"Keith, that's not an appropriate way to ask." Dr. Connor surveyed the room. The other hands in the room had recently been lowered as they likely had the same question as Laura. "Seeing as you seem to be the last one with a question, though, let us proceed."

"Have you heard the theories that since the primary problem with Earth was overpopulation, the Icarus was simply a way to murder ninety-nine percent of people and leave Earth to the rest?"

Dr. Connor smiled. "Now that's an interesting question, Keith, even though I disagree with how you asked it. In your view, are we dead?"

"I think we're ghosts of what we were. I agree that the Icarus was an elegant solution to a problem. However, I believe the problem was how do you commit a genocide of billions and still call yourselves humanity? Icarus allowed ninety-nine percent of the world to carry on in this shadow of life and not call the destruction of our bodies mass murder. Do the people in this room know where the name Icarus comes from? Do you, Dr. Connor?"

The room was silent. Dr. Connor loved a challenging discussion, and he found himself enjoying Keith for the first time all semester.

"Keith, I know the story of Icarus, and I expect many in this room would be able to answer if you weren't intimidating them. The story of Icarus dates to Greek mythology. Icarus was a young boy whose father built his wings out of feathers and wax. He flew too close to the sun when flying, melting the wax and plunging into the sea. Icarus was named after this because it's permanently flying, but unlike Icarus, it's safely hidden from the sun. A thousand feet underground is as far away from repeating the mistakes of Icarus as possible. Choosing a name from mythology was a tribute to our ability to dream and imagine. When it was named, people were less certain if our existence within Icarus would be as real as we thought it could be or more like dreaming. It seemed fitting."

"That's certainly the story," said Keith. "But the myth is less about what happened and more about the hubris of Icarus that led to his demise. His father warned Icarus that flying close to the sun would melt the wax, but Icarus felt this did not apply to him. He was so elated at his ability to fly, previously reserved for birds and the gods, that he didn't heed his father's warning. That's why he died, why he had to die. It's now our hubris, our belief that we can truly live without our bodies, that's being mocked by giving the mental storage center the name Icarus. The people who named it and inherited the earth are mocking us."

"I always love a good theory, Keith, and that's one I've heard about before. I can promise you that the only people left on Earth are a community of individuals around Icarus who take care of it. Which of the two scenarios you described would make you the happiest?"

"What do you mean?" Keith seemed stunned.

"Would you be happier if Earth was entirely uninhabitable, a wasteland of rolling storms, or do you find comfort in picturing an Earth recovered? Would you prefer it if we were all alone inside Icarus, or would you prefer that there was a beautiful community on the planet's surface, living in their bodies as nature intended? They would have achieved this life only because they had tricked the rest of us into existing simply as a connection of networks. Which of those two options do you find more upsetting?"

Keith paused. A rare interlude where he didn't have a remark at the ready. "I don't know, sir."

Dr. Connor looked at the rest of the room, and everyone was quiet. "Sarah, as everyone has had their questions asked, let us return to your second one."

"Thank you! My question is a little difficult to phrase. Our bodies are only manifestations of our thoughts so that we can interact, yet we are still restricted by the framework for historical bodies. Why are we still subject to biological restrictions?"

"I'm confused about what you mean, Sarah. All brains, since the dawn of mankind, have been nothing more than a series of connections. Why does it matter if they're digital or made of physical biology?"

"I guess, to ask it in a specific way, how come people still die and give birth when we no longer have a biological body that governs this? We each have this manifestation that allows our minds to interact comfortably, but why do the limitations remain? For example, why are some of us attractive and unattractive when our physical appearance in the room is created only by our minds?"

At this question, Dr. Connor paused. "That is a fascinating question, but I want to remind the class again that you should leave immediately if anyone feels uncomfortable about this topic. It's important for your health that you remain aware of this. Please remove yourself from this room at the slightest sign of any discomfort." The class was silent in their seats. No one moved.

"I can answer the part about death and appearance easily and scientifically. The connections in our brains degrade and misfire throughout our lives, and this is no different now. We no longer face diseases and afflictions without a biological body, but the degradation of the pathways that make up our minds cannot be stopped. We will die as we always have, but that mortality makes life precious and makes us human, so I am glad we did not lose it. Our appearance has always been directed by our genetics and our unconscious minds. Even during the centuries when we were born in a womb, there were parts of our brain directing how we looked that were always outside our control. Our programming continues to do this now, and it should not surprise anyone."

The class was silent as they listened to Dr. Connor. No one in the room made a sound.

"The question about attempting to impact change with our conscious minds is truly fascinating. Let's take the example of how humans still get pregnant in a world we have created entirely for ourselves. Without getting into some of the more technical aspects..." The professor had to pause as Keith coughed loudly and snickered. Like a ten-year-old boy, he had to tell everyone he knew how people got pregnant.

"Keith, I missed that. Did you have questions on this part?" Keith suddenly looked sheepish and shook his head.

"I'll continue then. Without getting into some of the more technical aspects, everything we understand is possible for that exact reason. Your brain knows when pregnancy is the normal response, and it manifests that response as it has for millions of years. Our brains evolved in parallel with our bodies, and this relationship was entrenched to the point that even without a body, a brain will continue to operate as if it had one. An interesting thing we've been looking at recently is whether people can condition their minds only to let them be pregnant for five months or six months and produce a fully formed baby. We no longer have the biological requirements of a nine-month pregnancy for a baby to form properly. Without this requirement, you would think it'd be easy to remove this step, but it's proving extremely difficult." Dr. Connor paused and surveyed the room to ensure no one looked sick. He knew he was saying too much but enjoyed the discussion as much as his students.

"We worked with one woman on this exact topic. She could comprehend and truly believe she didn't have to be pregnant for nine months. Her mind was fighting millions of years of evolution that told her differently. As a result of her efforts, she had the baby in two weeks. The belief that her physical body didn't need to conform to historical norms became embedded within her, and this belief grew like a weed. A week after she gave birth, we found her screaming at home; she had no legs. It was as if they'd never been a part of her. She'd done such a good job convincing her body that it wasn't real that she lost control of it. Her mind no longer believed in the body it had manifested. In the same way, you can become aware you're dreaming and never return to that previous ignorance. Her arms eventually fell off, and her skin slipped from her body. She became a pile of mush screaming at the air."

The class was in shocked silence. "That horror story can't be true," said Keith. "Why wouldn't she have died?"

"She didn't die because she knew exactly what she was: nothing more than data within the Icarus. Over and over, she convinced herself that her existence was simply a series of connections and pathways. Her mind knows it can exist for decades without degrading, so that's what it will do. She can't die until her mind lets her, and she knows that completely. What's left of her is kept in a small compartment at the laboratory until she's finally comfortable with the fact she no longer needs to exist or until her data degrades, whichever occurs first."

"Why wouldn't they take her offline from outside the system? Destroy the data that comprises her?"

Dr. Connor now realized that any previous beliefs by the students that this conversation was endorsed by the chancellor had now probably disappeared. "It's a good question, Keith. The chancellor and his team are extremely disapproving of attempts to push the boundaries of historical human living. Our experiments were conducted by a small group of doctors, professors, and scientists, and they weren't condoned by the establishment. We couldn't inform them of the experiments, so she couldn't be taken offline. I hold myself responsible for her situation and feel haunted by it."

Suddenly, in the corner of the room, Sarah excused herself and exited the classroom. It looked as if she was crying. It didn't surprise Dr. Connor that such a discussion could be traumatizing.

"That should probably conclude our class. This was as interesting as I thought it'd be. I'm happy to discuss your papers in my office hours starting Wednesday. Thank you for your keen questions. If what we discussed causes discomfort, please don't hesitate to reach out. I assure you that our lively discussion today and our risk-taking define what it means to be alive, so please do not have any confusion on that subject."

The class stood up and gave Dr. Connor a standing ovation. The students exited the school halls, and he shook each of their hands as they passed. He was exhausted now and sat down at his desk. He thought how stupid it was to talk to students about these things. He'd be gone soon, though, and felt his students needed to understand, or no one would be left who did. Perhaps they didn't need to, though. A part of him felt that a glossier version of their existence would be better. Perhaps only he needed to selfishly talk through the way things were now. Individuality was nothing more than a series of decisions; it helped him feel alive to make a wrong one occasionally.

He surveyed the empty classroom, knowing this would be his last semester teaching. He'd spent much of his life in this room. Looking over the desks, he noticed Sarah's bag beneath her seat. Twenty minutes had passed as he sat there thinking, and she still hadn't returned. He grabbed her bag and headed to the washroom to check on her. It wouldn't surprise him if the discussion had made her sick to her stomach.

"Sarah, are you in there?" He knocked on the door, but there was no reply. Dr. Connor put his ear against the door and could hear sobbing. "Sarah, I'm coming in."

Dr. Connor opened the door and saw Sarah standing with her back to him. "Is there anyone with you, Sarah?" No reply. She was hunched over with her face in her hands. "Sarah, it's okay to cry. It can be difficult to think through these things. That's why psychology is such an important pursuit these days. You're brave to devote your life to this. I'm going to come over there. I hope that's okay."

Slowly, he approached Sarah and put his hand on her shoulder. She turned and faced him. He realized she wasn't crying. She held her teeth and what appeared to be part of her lips in her hands. "What's happening?" she sobbed. Dr. Connor recoiled but quickly sprang into action.

"Sarah, I need you to focus on my face and think about how you're in this washroom with me right now. I'm going to call the authorities."

"What can they do?" Sarah screamed. "None of this is real!"

"They can help! It's a virus you have, and they can cure it." He knew it wasn't a virus, but they'd at least slow her mind so she wouldn't permanently lose her grip on reality.

Dr. Connor shouted into his watch, "A young woman is in the women's bathroom of King's College and is extremely ill; please hurry."

"There are no viruses!" said Sarah. "This happened to that woman you were talking about. I started thinking about that and couldn't stop! There's no reason for this physical projection of myself, whatever this body is." As she said this, her hands started to melt. He knew it was almost too late. She'd be stuck in a purgatory he'd seen before. He paused for a second, then put his hands around Sarah's head. He looked away and broke her neck. She collapsed motionless to the ground. He wondered if he'd done it in time. Sitting there in silence, he hoped no sound would come from her body. Hopefully, her mind still had enough of a grip on reality that it understood that snapping her neck was final. He waited a minute longer until he finally believed she was at peace. His only comfort was that he'd prevented her from being trapped in a private hell, perpetually aware that she couldn't die but unable to live. He cried beside her now until three men in suits arrived. He explained what had happened, and they excused themselves. Eventually, one of them returned and looked at Dr. Connor.

"The chancellor would like to see you personally. Come with us."

He was so distraught with what had occurred that the next two hours were a blur for Dr. Connor. Before he knew it, he was standing in a beautiful white room. A large wooden table in the center and the far wall contained a series of screens. The chancellor was a tall man with dark hair and sharp features. He stood in front of the screens and smiled at Dr. Connor. "I must say that you've done me a huge favor." Dr. Connor stared at him blankly.

"I and other administration members have debated for years whether people should be aware of the existence of Icarus or live without any knowledge of their reality. It was such a complicated decision that we arrived at this terrible happy medium, where we shared that truth with them but created an environment where they were prohibited from dwelling on it. Colleagues of mine, some of whom I believe are friends of yours, argued that people deserve to know. I've always been of the opposite opinion; that this knowledge is dangerous. Your little class proved me right in every regard." The chancellor approached Dr. Connor and put his hand on his shoulder. "Thanks to you, the Senate has unanimously approved my position to phase out all knowledge of the Icarus. We'll start with those who know the most; over time, we'll have entire generations that know nothing more about their life than what they see in front of them."

Dr. Connor sputtered, "You can't simply erase peoples' memories! It would be impossible to track where the memory is stored on each person's network." Dr. Connor realized he'd sentenced his entire class to death. His mouth was dry, and he was unable to speak.

“You’ll be taken offline immediately, and the same fate will meet your students. I apologize for this, but it’s best for everyone. There’s too great a risk that people won’t come to terms with their existence and that one day it creates widespread panic.”

Dr. Connor looked at the chancellor. “Why are you so concerned with order when you are more aware than anyone that we’re nothing more than data stored on a dying planet?”

The chancellor smiled. “Dr. Connor, if I ceased to believe my role here was important, it wouldn’t be long before I met the same fate as your student.”

Dr. Connor couldn’t argue with that. He knew his existence was coming to an end. “Sir, before you delete me, I have one question. Are there communities living on Earth in peace? Has the planet healed by putting all of us down here?”

The chancellor raised his eyebrow. “Would it make you happy if there were?”

“I honestly don’t know. That’s the beautiful thing about life; I can still surprise myself. Even after decades with ourselves, we still don’t know what we’ll do or how we’ll feel. That’s very real.”

The chancellor smiled at Dr. Connor and whispered into his watch. They looked at each other, and then Dr. Connor ceased to exist.

Ethics Score

"By refusing to answer the questions, the jury will be instructed to reference only your personal ethics score. In exercising this right, you will not be made aware of the score they have been provided by the court."

Gordon nodded. He smiled at the jury members, but they stared blankly. He looked at his wife and daughters as they watched from the gallery. His wife Jennifer smiled, but the smile was for the courthouse, not for him.

"Yes. I exercise my right not to comment on items of my character and instruct the jury to reference only my personal ethics score."

"In that case, I will proceed to my closing argument. Gordon Cole murdered Leslie Sims. We don't need to know why. The ethics score provided points to his general state of mind and moral tendencies. We have a key witness, James Sims, who saw the defendant leaving his house seconds before he returned home to find her murdered. Mr. Cole's fingerprints are all over the home, and Mr. Sim's ethics score should give you the utmost faith in his testimony. Give him the justice he deserves by believing him and by putting his wife's killer away."

Gordon sat with his lawyer in a small room. The jury had been out for almost an hour.

"What if this wasn't the correct approach?"

"I told you it wasn't the correct approach. You pay me all this money and then muzzle me." His lawyer threw his hands up in the air.

"I didn't think there was a chance of losing. We committed to keeping this secret, but the more they throw at us, the more I wonder. Maybe I'm holding on to something that doesn't exist anymore. I would rather be there to support my kids and have them hate me than be unable to help them from prison."

The door opened. "They are ready for you, Mr. Cole."

Gordon resumed his position. He turned around again to look at his family. It made him nervous, and he felt he had to memorize their faces.

"A jury of your peers, based on the evidence presented and an ethics score of 234, has decided that you are guilty."

Gordon erupted in anger. "That's not my ethics score! That score is reserved for rapists and scum. That can't be what was calculated for me! He did this. He did all of this!" He stepped out of the booth and ran toward James Sims. "I'm going to kill you! You killed her because she loved me, and you're smirking because you think both of us got what we deserve!" The security guards grabbed Gordon as he sputtered.

"You are a filthy cheater!" Jennifer shouted.

Gordon stopped moving and went limp in the guard's arms. "Baby, I did this for us. I didn't kill her. I didn't defend myself because I wanted to protect you and the kids. This was to protect you! It was an affair, but I never killed her!" He was screaming at anyone and everyone.

—— «» ——

Five Years Earlier

James Sims slammed his hand on the table. "It's genius. This is the revenue stream we have been waiting for. We don't need to produce anything. All we do is take what we have; everyone pays us for it. We create the demand simply by making people aware of the value here. Everyone will need it: governments, individuals, schools, universities, everyone."

Gary nodded and rubbed his chin with his hand. "Okay, go through it with me again before I take this to our board."

"We have more data than we know what to do with. We have a record of every message, image, and anything that goes through our system. Our company has more data on people than anywhere else. It's illegal to sell this data because it breaches privacy, but what if we aggregated the data first and then sold it? It would be aggregated so that no individual secret would even be close to visible. The only thing people would get is a set of numbers. It would be called the ethics score."

Gary was nodding and now, like any executive, wanted to prove to the room that he understood. "So, our software goes through everything anyone ever sends. It checks whether they are lying to their friends, cheating on their exams or their spouse, or, heaven forbid, even burying a body. It will even know if they were at a bar and got kicked out because, presumably, one of their friends will text them about it. The program will sift through everything to calculate a number between zero and a thousand, directly representing how ethical someone is. James, what was your team thinking for end purchasers?"

"That's the beauty of it. It's everyone. If you are a university, you will want to know. They can't spend all this time and money trying to reduce plagiarism, create safe campuses, and then say they won't pay to find out how ethical their applicants are. Premium dating sites will want it. Employers will want it. It will be like a credit score, except it can be applied to everything, and we will be the only people with access to it. It is a license to print money."

Gary was grinning. "We will show everyone that they need this. Gordon, are you on board?"

Gordon looked up from his phone and quickly put it in his pocket. He tried to hide the smile that had been playing across his face. "Apologies. It doesn't feel appropriate. Isn't it illegal to look at all that information? Everyone has a right to their privacy."

James leaned forward. "I've already done the preliminary sounding on this with the government. If we have software aggregating the data, they can find a way to get comfortable. Frankly, they understand how useful this would be, especially for them. It would speed up the courts and likely increase the number of correct verdicts by having this additional point of reference. Individuals will also start to think seriously about the collective weight of their actions. Corporations will be comfortable with it, too. Contracts are currently in a precarious middle ground, where they sometimes must terminate someone for something they dug up on social media, but there was no explicit description of that behavior in the contract. This would eliminate those wrongful dismissal cases with a catchall, as they could simply add to the contract that your score must remain above a certain level during your tenure. They will embrace this. Why are you so against it? Studies show that people cheat or steal less when they think someone is watching. This will drive that."

"It's too much power. A single number could drive how we are treated by the justice system and eventually by the broader community. The single number will be created by a company, by the people in this room."

"Aren't you glad you're in this room then?" The executive team shared a slight chuckle.

"We are a for-profit telecommunications company. I don't know if it should be up to us to label good and bad. This would be moral imperialism based on how we calculate scores, how we think people should live."

"What does it matter? I thought you had nothing to hide, Gordon." James smiled. The two men stared at each other as the world they were building brought them inevitably closer.

Thank You for Sharing

"Please describe when you and Jenn first met. We ask this at the end because it ties everything together. Our approach differentiates us."

A smile came across my face as I thought back. "I was getting coffee, and she was working. She asked me if I wanted room for cream, and I said no. She passed me the coffee, and I couldn't take my eyes off her, so I bumped into the counter as I turned and spilled everywhere. I grabbed some napkins and started wiping the floor. She quickly started helping me."

I adjusted myself in the chair and looked over at Dr. Young. "Did you get that?"

"Yes, thank you. What next?"

"I asked her if she'd like to visit a restaurant and see me spill stuff there instead. She giggled and said if I could save that for six o'clock, she would love to meet me at the restaurant around the corner. We haven't gone a day since without talking. Ten years."

"Thanks, William. That's it. The only thing left is for you to picture the first time you two were intimate. Please just picture it, and we will monitor you. That will give us everything we need."

"Is that necessary? I came here because your team is the most professional. I don't want the feelings about my wife being used in that way."

Dr. Young peered out from behind the monitoring machine.

"Listen, the Cephalopods will only pay for the purest feelings. Pleasure is the easiest. Hell, you can get that through medication. Pain is easy. Many companies in the universe produce that feeling against people's will and package it. Love and loss, particularly voluntary loss, take time, thought, and architecture. They are beautiful stories with highs and lows, and, for that reason, they fetch the highest price. That is what we do here. Everything we ask for is an important part of that."

I nodded and thought about the first time we were together. There was part I kept to myself. That is all I would have. I would keep that forever. "Do you have everything you need? I should get home." My voice was shaky.

He reviewed his monitor. "That's excellent work. Based on what we've received today, we expect you will not want to go through with this when the time comes. For that reason, you're required to sign the below contract. I apologize for this part; it's always uglier than it needs to be, but we wouldn't get the correct product if we omitted this step."

I scanned to the bottom of the contract. *The undersigned must have completed the act by midnight local time. Any delay beyond the scheduled time voids the act. Any explanations void the act. Any removal of the monitoring device is deemed equivalent to the above. Punishments for contract violation include but are not limited to, a $500,000 fine and imprisonment. The fine is extended to all family members.*

I paused and reread it as Dr. Young spoke.

"The money will be deposited in Jenn's account a day after you leave. Depending on final readings, it will be anywhere from a million to two million. I can tell you that your pre-qualifiers are some of the best we've seen in years. It wouldn't surprise me if it approaches two."

He now put his hand on my shoulder. "They're going to have excellent lives, William. The types of lives people dream of. All thanks to you. You are providing for them the way a husband and father should."

I nodded and signed the document.

Dr. Young's tone changed. He spoke quickly and with excitement. "We'll remove the implant as soon as you are done. It's been a pleasure doing business with you. You already mentioned this, but are you certain you don't want any of the compensation in your account?"

I shook my head. "None. Every penny to them."

"Right, you are." He grinned. "This will be in the two-million-dollar range. Might even fetch a premium beyond that." He reached out to shake my hand, but I simply nodded, thanked him, and exited.

I walked around in a daze. I was scared about too much time at home, but I also knew I should be spending every remaining second there, memorizing their faces. It was dark when I walked in the door. Jenn was reading a book on the couch, nestled under an old torn blanket. Only the small lamp beside the couch was on. She looked up and smiled.

"There you are. I was starting to worry. Billy almost couldn't fall asleep without you. He was worried you'd be up all night since the two of you didn't read your bedtime stories. It was so cute. He thinks the stories are for you to fall asleep."

"I had to put in an extra shift, but I got overtime, so we'll be able to pay utilities."

Jenn sighed. "Thank you for doing that. I know how tough it's been. We'll make it work, though; we always do. We're a team. Do you want to watch a movie?"

"Let's just sit." I found a spot next to her on the couch. She put her book down and rested her head on my chest. I smelled the top of her head and breathed deeply.

I looked at the clock. It was already eleven. My hands were sweaty. "Jenn..." I couldn't get the words out.

She turned and looked at me with her big eyes. "Bedtime? My turn for a story?"

"No." I clenched my fists and pushed the words out. "I'm leaving you."

"Is this because I didn't split that cookie with you yesterday?"

I didn't laugh. "You won't see me again."

"Is this a joke? We're a team."

I stood up and started walking toward the door. She got up and grabbed my arm. "Everything's okay. What is this?"

"Nothing is okay! We can't afford to send Billy to the same school as his friends. We can't afford rent. What are we doing? I have to leave this."

Jenn was crying now and holding onto my arm.

"It's for us. I promise it's for us. I need to go. Now!" My other hand was on the doorknob.

I heard the feet on the stairs. His excitement made him sound larger than he was. I knew I should leave right then before I saw him. I started to turn but stopped; I had to see his face come around the corner one more time. A couple more steps, and his head bobbed into eyesight. His blond hair was disheveled, and he had brought his stuffed animal for the trip downstairs. I smiled at him, and he smiled back.

"Daddy, you need story time to sleep?"

I couldn't stop my tears. "Hey, kid." I stepped forward and hugged him tightly. At that moment, I wasn't leaving. This was everything, and then I remembered the contract. I squeezed his shoulders and looked him in the eyes. "I have to go on a trip. You take care of your mother. The two of you are going to have an amazing life."

Jenn was on her knees. "You can't leave him, too! If you don't love me anymore, that's fine; we can work that out in the morning; just tuck your son into bed. I can sleep on the couch, or you can do whatever you need. Just don't leave!" She sobbed uncontrollably in deep gasps.

"Why you going Daddy?"

"Please go upstairs, Billy." My lips were shaking, and I couldn't get the words out. "Only your mom needs to be here for this."

Billy grabbed my leg. "Don't cry. You told me hugs make it better."

I had to leave immediately; my heart couldn't take any more.

"Get off, Billy!" I shouted in a way I never had.

"Don't go." He hugged tighter. I shook my leg, and he fell to the floor, crying.

"What is wrong with you?" Jenn screamed. She embraced Billy and turned him away from me. "Just go if it's so important to you!"

Their faces were blurred as tears filled my eyes. "You are everything to me." I slammed the door and ran into the street. A blue van pulled up in front of the house, and I got in.

"Congratulations, sir. We have already received bids for this emotional sequence as high as three million. Your family is very lucky."

Verdict

Nick Vale entered the room through the giant golden doors. He walked past dozens of empty seats, moving slowly to ensure the judges understood how old and tired he was. It was only him and the judges in the courthouse today. Given the circumstances, the court had granted Nick a private hearing. They pretended this was a courtesy to Nick; he knew the real reason was that they couldn't afford to have this publicized. Nick would have preferred a public hearing. He had been alive for almost three centuries and, in that time, whenever he'd seen a desire to keep something private, it was due to a preference for reduced accountability.

Nick approached the solitary chair sitting in front of the panel. The five judges were already seated behind their black podiums, looking down at him. Nick knew Judge Randal and Judge Meyer. He didn't know the other three personally. Judge Dewitt would lead the dialogue, and it appeared he was preparing to speak.

"We're here today because Judge Randal and Judge Meyer asked that we hear your case. Due to their relationship with you, they'll be required to abstain from voting. The three remaining members are sufficient for a quorum. I hope you understand how unique it is to sit in front of the panel at your age. You're only two hundred and sixty years old. Four decades from the minimum permitted age and in good health and social standing."

Nick tried to let only respectful comments escape his pursed lips. "I know. I appreciate you taking the time today."

The judges didn't look up from their notes. They whispered briefly, and then Judge Dewitt continued.

"We've reviewed the results of your psychological evaluation. There are no conditions or predispositions that would suggest you haven't submitted this request in a rational state of mind. We'll, therefore, proceed with your initial statement. Why do you want to die, Mr. Vale?"

Nick stood up. He wasn't a man to get nervous; he'd been a top surgeon for over a century. He wondered how to form the words in a way they'd understand. It was so deeply personal.

"Mr. Vale?"

"Yes, my apologies. I simply feel I'm done living life as it was meant. I'm not creating anymore. I'm not building. I'm simply a caretaker of the life I built. I have six beautiful generations below me now. They all bear my last name." Nick's voice grew louder as he gained confidence. "I built a career and assisted with some of the most important medical advances in the past few centuries. Those things are behind me now. All I could do now is make a mistake that would discredit what I've done. A single mistake could tear down what I've built. I live in fear now of destroying this amazing life. The greatest happiness a person can achieve is from creating, while the greatest sadness comes from destroying something. I've built so much that there's no way that, over the next four decades, there can be more creating than destroying. I'm tired and scared, and I deserve to be granted permission to die after everything I've done for our country."

Nick finished his speech and stood waiting. Judge Randal, a friend, smiled at him and nodded. Judge Dewitt looked directly at him.

"Mr. Vale, we appreciate the frankness of your answer. Some men and women work in mines for three hundred years and aren't permitted a chance to die. They work each day, appreciating their role as citizens. The minimum death age was created for a reason. Our country has trillions of dollars of debt that amounts to millions for each citizen. If everyone doesn't put in his or her three hundred working years, we'll never be able to grow out of this debt. Other countries have similar policies or worse. Why do you believe you're exempt from the burden that falls on your fellow citizens?"

Nick slammed his hands down. "Does the panel believe life has a purpose even if there's no happiness? Shouldn't we re-evaluate the path we're putting people on?"

"It's not the purpose of our panel to opine on the type of society we live in. Our role is to evaluate, on a case-by-case basis, whether an individual is permitted to die early. We almost exclusively hear cases that result from health conditions. It is so upsetting that those would give anything to live your life. They only come before us because they can't deal with the pain. For this reason, your submission in front of this panel is distasteful. Many of the greatest lives ever lived throughout humanity were ones filled with unhappiness. I don't believe in your statement that individual happiness is paramount. All of us are contributing to something larger than ourselves every day. That is what society is, and society requires more of you!"

Nick was furious. "A man shouldn't have to live to three hundred! What we've created here isn't natural. The system should serve us, not the other way around!"

"I'm sorry, but you haven't presented a compelling case today, and we aren't willing to set a dangerous precedent. Your request is denied. I would also like to remind you of the punishment that extends to family members in the case a suicide occurs."

Nick nodded. He looked as defeated as he felt. He was usually the type of man who would thank them for their time, but that wasn't in him anymore. He stood up and exited the room in a daze. He looked more fragile now than he'd tried to look at the start. Judge Randal caught up with him in the hallway outside the courthouse.

"I'm sorry about that, Nick."

Nick didn't reply. Judge Randal put a hand on Nick's shoulder.

"Nick, they're looking for doctors in the perimeter colonies. The colonies are well beyond the historical system boundaries. Things are dangerous out there. There isn't the law and order we see back home. People die, doctors die. Most importantly, though, people there need help. I'll put you in touch with my friend who operates the transport ships that head there. You should go. I think you'll find what you're looking for, one way or another."

The Last Sacrifice to Freyr

"The man sitting in front of us is a murderer. This is simple. There were no grand ambitions, no net benefit, to what he did. Don't let him persuade you otherwise. Nothing can justify the mass murder he committed." The prosecutor paused. He'd grown increasingly theatrical as he addressed the courtroom. He turned and faced Lang Cooney.

"At what point during the Aldrin voyages did you know you were sending people to die?"

Lang raised his head. His face had a strength that was still apparent despite old age. "It was before the thirty-first voyage that I was made aware of the complications. Fifteen voyages followed. The program launched almost fifty thousand people in total. Each one left with the hope of introducing humanity to the universe. They had no idea they didn't have a chance." Lang's open admission was a surprise. The silence that followed made everyone aware of the noise outside; the riots were growing.

"You admit to murdering all those individuals?"

Lang bristled. He'd been composed for most of the trial, a tremendous feat when, outside the courthouse, a mob shouted his name.

"You're a child if you don't understand what I did. Every individual on those ships was there for the same reason that I chose to keep sending them. We all believed in something larger than ourselves: a future for humanity beyond darkness and despair. We were saving people, but it wasn't in the way everyone thought. Look around now. The world burns. I was doing everything in my power to hold this off."

"You're the sole reason for these mobs! They want justice for your actions. You betrayed the trust our citizens had in their government!" The prosecutor ran his hands through his hair. He was aware the world was watching.

Lang looked at the prosecutor and then turned to address everyone in the court. "You're naive if you believe my death will satisfy the people outside these doors. We've all lost something we can never get back."

—— «» ——

Fifteen Years Earlier

Commander Lang Cooney stood behind his desk; he'd seen too much action to be comfortable sitting down in his lifetime. The office window he stared at faced the internal launch bay; everything outside the window was his responsibility. A stark contrast existed between the beautifully wood-paneled office and the grand window revealing sparks, steel, and spaceships. In the center of the launch bay, the crew of the thirty-first Aldrin voyage was preparing for launch. The target for the voyage was planet C-07.

During the last three decades, the pursuit of finding intelligent life had consumed humanity; people wanted to finally be acknowledged by the nothingness that surrounded them. Every year the federation launched a new ship to the most promising planet. An entire community was aboard and ready to establish life on the planet in the event it turned out to be suitable. The hope was to find life either directly on the planet or indirectly by being in proximity to intelligent life in that part of the universe. Citizens everywhere believed it was only a matter of time.

Lang was deep in thought when Professor Kevin Kern ran into his office.

"Sir, there's a problem with the Aldrin program. I've been studying the systems we're headed to, and there isn't enough dark matter in that part of the universe to slow expansion at a reasonable rate. We previously overestimated how much there is. On cosmologically large scales, certain target planets have reached an acceleration away from our point of reference faster than any of our possible means of travel." Kevin rapidly tapped his hand against his leg and stared at Lang as if expecting an informed response.

Lang stared blankly. Before Kevin could start back up again, Lang said, "Stop. What did you come here to say?"

Kevin paused.

"Sir, the universe is expanding and has been doing so throughout time. It's expanding faster and faster. Smaller units, our solar system, for example, are bound together by gravity, but these distinct units grow farther and farther apart from their equivalents in other parts of the universe. Other solar systems, such as the ones we target on the Aldrin voyages, are moving farther away from us with each second. This expansion is delayed by gravity. Gravity is exerted by normal matter and dark matter. If there's a lack of matter, expansion continues with minimal restrictions. That's what's happening. Even if they left today, our ships could never reach planet C-07 because it's speeding away faster than they can travel. There are certain places that we simply didn't get to in time. We'll never reach them now. We'll never know what they contain."

Lang thought about what Kevin had said. It didn't take him long.

"You're telling me that if I launch this voyage, I'm sending people to their deaths?"

"With certainty. They will be in a metal can, traveling toward something they can never reach. That will be their existence until they die or go insane. I know it's not what you want to hear, but we missed our chance. There might have been life there, but we'll never know. There is a lot science can do, but we will never get this back."

"We're too late," Lang said quietly. He stood there with none of his usual bravado. "When would we have had to launch to make it in time?"

"Sir, I don't think there's any value in dwelling on what could have been," Kevin replied.

"When?" Lang repeated.

"Two weeks. Two weeks earlier, we'd have been able to find out what was on that planet. It's impossible now."

Lang was silent. He suddenly seemed smaller, almost fragile, and the strength that had radiated from him had disappeared.

"I know this must be a terrible blow for you. That's why I wanted to tell you before I told the rest of the team. This should give you time to process it before we announce and cancel the launch."

"You mean only the two of us know?"

"Yes, I only finished the calculations today. Over the last century, we have become so interested in the existence of dark matter that the absence of it hasn't been contemplated. As I said, I wanted to tell you before it got out."

"I appreciate that, and it was the right thing to do... I hope you understand that you can never tell anyone."

"Sir..."

"Kevin, you're the most intelligent man I know. You must have noticed what these launches mean to the world. They've given us something to believe in, a common purpose."

"It isn't worth lives."

"It's worth everything!" Lang slammed his hand on the table. "Did you know the global suicide rate is a tenth of what it was when I was your age? Humanity still has problems, but everyone, the good and evil, the healthy and sick, the rich and poor, wants a chance to see the next launch and find out if we're not alone. Humanity needs someone or something to look back at us and say we exist; to acknowledge what we've done. We need a legacy."

"A legacy? We have a legacy. We've accomplished unbelievable things." Kevin gestured at the launch bay. "Our ancestors could only dream of what we've built."

"We have no legacy and no answers. If we don't find something else in this universe, something to acknowledge us, we're left with nothing. A couple of million years, and then maybe we cease to exist. We'll have been nothing but a spec in this great story. Our search for intelligent life has made everyone strive a little harder. Crime has dropped. We think of ourselves as a collective instead of individuals. My grandfather said they still taught children about great men like Napoleon when he was in school. Even by the time I was in school, names like that were all but forgotten. There's too much history, too much to learn about the past, and too many people have come and gone. Humanity has become expansive to the point that no single individual can leave a legacy. Our only hope is a collective legacy."

Kevin was quiet for a long time and stared at Lang.

"I understand what you're saying, that you need humanity to be measured."

"What?"

"I had a professor when I was younger who always told us that, at the quantum level, reality doesn't exist if you aren't measuring it. Only once you observe it through measurement is its existence confirmed. You're worried that humanity doesn't exist until we find someone or something out there to observe us."

"Yes," Lang replied. "That's exactly it." A sadness and a silence had fallen over the two men.

"I can't lie to people, Lang," Kevin said. "We need to tell them. I agree with everything you said, but I believe people will understand that there are no more missions. They can handle it."

"You can't tell them! All they'll understand is that we're utterly alone in this universe. The world will burn. We have no purpose if we aren't searching for answers, and this is the last remaining question." As Lang said this, he moved closer to Kevin.

"Are you sure this isn't your legacy you're talking about, Lang?" Kevin's voice was shaky and almost whispered. "You never married and never had kids. This is all you have. Are you certain you're speaking on behalf of humanity?"

"I know that I'm not doing this for me, and I believe you when you say you won't be able to lie. I want you to understand that I'm not a monster, but I've always understood, from my time in the army, that sometimes the one needs to be sacrificed to save the many, even when it's a friend."

Lang put his massive hands on the sides of Kevin's head, and the two men cried as they looked at each other. They understood how lonely the world had become. Fifty billion people spread across the solar system, yet the silence was suddenly unbearable. With a quick movement, Lang broke Kevin's neck.

Four days later, the thirty-first Aldrin voyage launched. Citizens everywhere cheered. Lang sat with the widow and Kevin's son at Kevin Kern's funeral. Lang cried in their arms and told them he couldn't believe such an accident could happen at his facilities. The machines had continuously been operated safely, and he took full responsibility for the freak accident that took the life of a father and husband. Saying it was his fault caused another wave of tears.

Lang looked down at Kevin's son and wiped his face. "David, you're being so strong. You're doing such a good job comforting your mother. Your father would have been so proud."

David looked up at Lang.

"I need to be the man of the house now for when we meet the aliens. I want to impress them. I only wish my dad could have met them."

—— «» ——

Present Day

Lang finished speaking to the court. He no longer seemed defensive, simply sad. The prosecutor brought a screen from one of his assistants. Lang couldn't see what was on it but assumed it was a critical part of his closing arguments. Lang didn't care anymore. The rumble outside grew louder. Gunshots could suddenly be heard in the halls outside the great court. Lang stood up.

The prosecutor looked furious. "The guards have control of the situation, and this commotion is no excuse for a recess!" Lang didn't reply. This time, he stared at the broadcasting camera. His eyes were wet.

"It's been an honor to serve as your commander. Please find something that unites us."

The sound of bodies against the doors of the great courtroom started to scare the people in attendance. Everyone in the room pushed to the front, away from the noise, and toward Lang. Lang stood there and continued to look at the broadcasting camera.

"This isn't an opportunity for you to gain sympathy!" The prosecutor could barely be heard against the rising noise.

The mob broke through the doors. The national security team had been unable to contain them. Lang watched as the prosecutor and others were shot by accident in the crossfire. The prosecutor dropped his screen. Lang could now see the photo, a picture of David Kern. The last time Lang had seen him had been at the funeral. It was too hard for Lang to see him after that. In this photo, he was much older; it was almost ten years later, and he proudly wore his Aldrin voyage personnel uniform. Lang stood there for two more seconds, looking at it before he was shot in the head. The courthouse burned.

Unlocked

The man slid the photo across the table, a picture of me in a place I'd never been. I was sure I hadn't been there because the place couldn't exist. Yet there I was, with my usual smile, standing in front of a tower of silver and a landscape of red dirt. The most unnerving thing was that he was also in the photo; it showed me with my arm around this man I'd never met.

"Why'd you photoshop this? What is this?"

He introduced himself as Ajax, a sales representative who wanted to discuss our company's printer needs. Salespeople are always quirky, but this was the first time I felt genuinely uncomfortable. Ajax smiled. "That's a picture of me and a man named John Auger." I looked at the photo again. There was no confusion; it was me.

"Ajax, I want you to leave. I believe you arranged this meeting under false pretenses." I couldn't figure out what he wanted.

"No matter what I try, this meeting never goes smoothly. I thought showing you a picture might work. You're curious by nature. Don't you want to know about this twin of yours?" He smiled.

He was weirdly right. I was curious. It was the way he said "twin." I was born with a twin who died from a genetic heart defect. His choice of words seemed prescient. "What do you mean, 'twin'?"

"There's the man I know!" He shouted as if speaking to an old friend. "I'm going to be perfectly honest. The man in the photo was more than a twin to you. He and I were best friends a long time ago. Can we take a walk to that park behind the building?"

As if an outside observer, I watched myself say yes. We took the elevator down and walked out the front door. We sat down on a bench without exchanging words. Finally, I asked, "Who is John Auger?"

He reached into his briefcase and pulled out more photos. I was in every one of them, or John was. "That question has been asked many times before. John Auger is your genetic equal. He even had the same problems in his foot. His left eye had that twitch."

Those were my secrets. "How'd you know that?"

"It's because you were designed to be exactly like him. Same genetics."

"What do you mean 'designed'? I know who my parents were. There's no confusion there."

"Your parents are still your parents. The design had to begin long before that." He paused. "It's good you have an open mind. Many people could not think about what I'm about to describe. Earth was created for one purpose; my people and I required a genetic equivalent of John Auger. I know that sounds shocking but think of it as a large experiment, as if you were synthesizing something. The only difference is you probably view Earth as an infinitely complex system. It's certainly complex but the inputs are finite. Controlling all those variables, you can see how we should be able to produce identical results a high percentage of the time."

He was lucky I loved thought experiments. "You're saying billions of years of evolution was an experiment?

He nodded and added, "With very targeted results."

"It makes no sense. How could you have known this man so long ago and still be alive?"

"Time is relative. There are beings whose lives have already come and gone while we sit here. The life of a fly seems very normal to a fly."

I had no interest in asking what he meant by that. "If this is all true, to what end did you need a genetic equivalent of John Auger?"

"Where I come from, we have genetically sealed locks. Only specific individuals can open certain things. No amount of force can change that. John Auger created something very important that our entire world desperately needs. Unfortunately, he then met an accidental death. Before he died, he locked the item. We need him, you, to open it."

He seemed very serious. "Ajax let's say you are from somewhere else. With infinite technology to engineer Earth, why not simply clone this man you want?"

"The lock would never open for a clone. It's not the same. That's counterfeiting."

I was silent as I thought about what he was saying.

"If you don't believe me, let me show you."

"Okay." I thought I was agreeing to something small, perhaps an additional photo. Ajax pulled two silver wristbands from his pocket and put them on my wrists. I noticed he wore identical bands. The bands on my wrists began heating up. I went to pull them off, but the pain was gone. We were no longer in the park. I now stood in front of the tower from the photo.

My vision spun, and my head hurt. I felt sick. I started screaming, but Ajax didn't even respond, so, eventually, like a child, I stopped. The whole thing was so weird that even normal reactions seemed out of place. Perhaps I was in shock.

He pointed. "Follow me."

We stepped into the tower. Inside was a clean white room. On the far wall, a glass display shifted between images.

Ajax led me to the display. "It's simple. We pull up your profile, and then the computer scans you. That's all that's required, and it saves a great many lives. That's why we've gone to all this trouble. You would be doing us a great service today."

Everything seemed like a dream now. I walked up to the panel. A serene female voice greeted me. "Welcome back, John. You asked me to send a message to you. Here it is."

Suddenly, I was looking at myself in the glass panel. It was a video of John Auger standing where I was now. He looked at me and said, "Dooot, dooot," and then collapsed on the floor. The video stopped playing. It was terrifying to see him fall. I knew this was when he died.

Ajax did not look surprised. "I apologize if that's traumatizing. We have no idea what the message means. John was unstable near the end." He looked at me with a seriousness that contrasted with his earlier warmth. "Do you know what it means?"

"No idea," I lied.

"You need to open it now." The friendliness in his voice was gone.

"How do I open it? There are no handles."

"All you need to do is think that you want it open, and the computer will recognize that. You must be uncertain right now."

A cold sweat covered me as I thought about what Ajax said earlier. "You said no matter how many times you tried; this meeting never went well? How many times have you brought someone... me... here?"

Ajax looked at me coldly. “More than once.”

I thought about what that meant. “If I’m here, it means they decided not to open it.”

“There were complications.”

I now understood the answer to the question I was about to ask. “What happens if I don’t open it?”

“Then we’ll reproduce your genetic equivalent until someone does. We’ll start fresh with Earth. If you open it, though, we no longer need to. You and the world you know will be left alone.”

I thought about what he said. He was about to speak again when we heard the female voice. “John, your storage box is unlocked.” Ajax looked surprised and then ecstatic. A large box, about two feet wide, now started to appear out of the wall. Without introduction, several men came into the room, grabbed the box, and left. “Thank you for your help today. It will change our world.” He embraced me, put the bands on my wrist, and before I knew it, I was back at the bench. I was alone.

I walked through the park in a daze. When I was a young boy, I had a speech impediment. My cousins would tickle me, and no matter how hard I tried to say “don’t,” it always came out as “dooot.” It made for cute family videos years later: a little boy giggling uncontrollably and appearing to repeat “Do it.” But I remember desperately wanting them not to. I saw those same eyes in John Auger. I knew what he was trying to tell me. Despite my genetic similarities with that man, I’d been unable to die for what he’d died to protect. I wondered what I’d done. I wondered what in my life had made me worse or made him better.

One Month

Robert Jacques lay in bed with his eyes on the ceiling. He'd yet to fall asleep. It no longer mattered; he knew the morning was approaching. At any moment, his mom would knock on his door. She was probably conflicted between a terrible fear that he'd sleep through his alarm and wanting to wait as long as possible before knocking to show him that he was independent. It was the type of intense but simple struggle that could only be contained within a loving mother.

In the days leading up to this, he'd thought his mother was more nervous than he was. After being unable to sleep all night, he realized it was probably a coin flip. As Robert lay there, he wished he had treasured a little more yesterday and the day before. He hadn't understood at the time how much better they were than today. The knock came.

"Honey, we made your favorite breakfast! Come down whenever you're ready." Her voice was strained and full of love. He recognized that tone. When he was younger, until twelve, he had asked for a Challenger robot every year for Christmas. The toy came with a gun, and you could play hide and seek with the robot. The robot was able to run, jump, and hide; it put up a real challenge for a young kid. When you shoot it, the robot will make a tremendous noise with sparks and fall. You could then simply press a button to reset it and you were ready to play again. Every year, his mom said, "We'll see what we can do, dear," in that same strained voice. It was only once he was older and realized that they couldn't afford it that he stopped asking.

He lay there a little while longer and then replied only to try to prevent her from coming in.

"I'll be right down." And then he added something, as much for himself as for her. "I'm very excited! Thank you!"

His bag was packed, and his favorite outfit was folded at the foot of his bed. He had never worn this "favorite" outfit before. His mom had spent weeks picking it out and begging the store owner to sell it to her at a discount. He looked at it and reviled it. Most of his anger was because he thought it looked good; ten times better than all his previous clothes. It was a gray collared shirt with a shimmer that changed with respect to the surroundings. It was tremendously light, but the fabric appeared to have a weight to it that forced it to hug his frame and never wrinkle. He looked at himself in the mirror, sighed, grabbed his duffel, and headed downstairs.

"Oh, you look lovely!" His mom ran up and hugged him. "Don't you think he looks lovely, dear?" His father sat at the table and had yet to look up.

Robert joked with his father, "If Dad never looks, he won't have to tell the guys at the plant how lame I looked."

His father glanced up briefly, winked, and returned to focusing on breakfast. Robert didn't have the same gruffness as his father, but they shared a sense of humor and a streak of defiance.

His father finally looked up. "Laura, I still don't understand why you insist he participates in the Tests. Doug's son isn't going, and neither is Ned's daughter. Their kids are starting at the plant right away."

His mom put her hands on Robert's shoulders and squeezed. "It's important he sees everyone from the different provinces. He deserves to choose what type of life he has."

"There's no choice!" His father banged his hand on the table. "Giving the perception of choice has always been just as good at sustaining peace as giving choice. Why would we participate in that charade? Remember, son, the happiest man is the man with nothing to worry about. You're too young to understand what's valuable in life, so don't let them tell you what is."

Laura smiled. "You're always surprisingly eloquent, dear. For someone against the higher professions, you could have succeeded at one."

"My father never let me go. Instead, I started work at the plant the day I turned fifteen. The best thing that ever happened to me. I've met people from Auger, Troy, and Volga. I promise you this: they're less happy than us. You'll understand that soon, Robert."

Robert nodded at his father. He honestly didn't know how he felt about the Aptitude Tests. Going to work at the plant with his father didn't interest him, but he didn't want to leave home to go to Temple City either. He wasn't very hungry and cleaned up his plate. With his duffel over his shoulder, he walked to the front hall of their house. His mother quickly shuffled after him, with his father trailing behind.

He smiled at the two of them as they stood there. "Well, this is it, I'll see you both in a month."

Robert's mother quickly embraced him; she did not intend to let go. He could hear her sniffling over his shoulder. He stepped back and put his hands on her shoulders.

"Don't cry. It's only a month."

She paused and wiped tears from her eyes. She squeezed Robert's shoulders again and whispered in his ear, "You don't know how strong you are, but they soon will. Everyone will."

She embraced him quickly once more. He then hugged his father.

"Have a good time, son. See you soon."

His mother couldn't stop crying but tried to compensate by giving her typical directions. "Okay, love, I can see the van waiting outside. Make sure you have everything. If anything happens, don't hesitate to call. You can come home at any time."

Robert nodded, turned around, and walked out to the waiting van. He prepared to greet other kids as he opened the side door, but the van was empty. He sat in the middle and put his duffel on his lap to make the seats next to him look inviting.

The driver muttered a muffled "good morning" as they pulled away. Robert gave a final wave to his parents as they stood in the doorway.

The van quickly switched to the priority government lane on the highway. It was faster than any vehicle he'd been in.

He called out to the driver. "Who else we picking up?" There was a pretty girl in the neighborhood that would have been about his age. He knew nothing about her but hoped she would be at the Tests.

"No one, kid. You're the only stop in this province. You're the first time we've been to this province in five years."

Robert's face fell. His dad was right, he had no business being here. The driver must have noticed Robert's disappointment because he changed his tone.

"I grew up only a few blocks from you. A couple of decades ago, but nonetheless."

Robert's only thought was the guy was messing with him. He was an intelligent kid, and he fully expected everyone from Temple City and the central provinces to give him a hard time. The driver continued.

"I'm serious. Do you know that old bar on Ross Street? I'm not certain what it's called now, but it used to be called The Armadillo."

Robert knew the bar. "They still call it that."

The driver laughed. "Doesn't surprise me one bit. That place is stuck in time. There was a side door that was broken and permanently ajar. As kids, we'd sneak in that way. They never fixed it in all the years we went."

This time, it was Robert's turn to laugh. He knew the exact door. "I'm glad they never fixed it. I took advantage of that a few weeks ago."

The driver smiled. "You're alright. I'm surprised you didn't believe I grew up there. I thought you'd have recognized me from a *Don't Serve* sign there."

The two of them laughed. "Hey, kid. You'll see a lot of new stuff at the Tests and meet many new people. It's important to remember that you can do much worse than your life. I've been driving kids for years, and for some years, I get the central provinces. Those kids aren't happy either. Believe me. Everyone has problems. You're the first kid I've enjoyed or that asked me anything, so you get full points from me. I'm sorry they aren't worth anything for the Tests."

As the driver spoke, Robert looked out the window. They'd arrived on the outskirts of Temple City, and he was mesmerized. It was unlike anything he'd ever seen. The buildings were white and silver. They twisted in and out of each other in a race to get higher. It reminded him of snakes in a pit jostling to gain position. The van approached the large walls that were remnants of the Century Wars. Parts of the wall had been commandeered by commerce, with shops and restaurants, but there remained large uninterrupted stretches. It was as if the individuals inside still didn't feel safe enough to take them down.

The driver lowered the window to talk to the man at the gate.

"I'm taking this one to the Tests." He pointed at Robert in the back, and Robert gave a weird smile that validated nothing.

The man at the gate leaned forward. "Good luck, kid. Enjoy your stay in Temple City."

They passed through the gates. Robert now had his face pressed against the window of the van. There were so many sights and sounds. Terraces overflowing with people. Fountains and canals. Gardens that appeared as if they'd drop ripe fruit on your plate as you ate at the restaurant nearby. The people were the most interesting, though. He'd already noticed five of the most beautiful girls he'd ever seen. They had a glow and excitement he hadn't seen before. He hated himself for thinking that. It was probably what time and money did to a person. These girls weren't burdened by the responsibilities people faced in his neighborhood. As he was thinking through how unfair this was, he saw her. Bright eyes and blonde hair. She was walking backward while facing and talking to her mom. Her hands were expressive, and she was passionate about what she was saying. He couldn't hear her, but it didn't matter; he knew instantly he'd love it.

The van stopped at a light, and he sat there, fixated, hands pressed against the window. She suddenly turned to look at him. He kept staring. He thought the windows were more tinted than they were. Eventually, he realized she was looking right at him. He oddly wasn't embarrassed. She gave him a scolding but complicit smile and looked away.

"Be careful around Temple City girls." The driver had noticed his infatuation. "They look nice, but they are dragons. That's Melissa Burgess. Her father runs the Tests."

All Robert heard was "Melissa." He was still thinking about her when the van stopped. They'd pulled up in front of a massive building. He thought it was a monument as they approached. It was a white cube with no discernible windows, but there was a shimmer. The size and apparent simplicity of it shocked him. He realized he couldn't see where it ended; it extended right as far as he could see. It was partially covered by other buildings, but they appeared to be built around it, or it was built through them. The driver turned around. "Here you are, Aptitude Tests Plaza."

Suddenly, Robert was nervous in a way that was unusual for him. "Where do I go now?"

"Head in through those doors. There'll be a desk where you declare yourself; they will take it from there. This thing runs like clockwork now. You barely notice the four thousand other kids, which is amazing. Good luck. We'll cross paths again."

Robert lightly smiled. "Yep, when you take me back home at the end." He threw his bag over his shoulder and extended his hand to the driver. "Thank you for the ride. I don't know your name, though."

The driver smiled. "That's nice kid. Not many people ask their driver's name." There was a long pause, but the man said nothing more.

Robert simply nodded, and they shook hands.

He stepped out of the van and shielded his eyes from the glare of the building. He could see groups of kids getting out of vans nearby. They all laughed together and jostled as they headed into the main entrance. Robert followed behind, but he walked alone. He funneled into one of the lines leading to a central concierge. Children waved at friends. Some individuals had so many bags they needed assistants to carry them, or they had brought so many bags because they had assistants. He watched it all in silence.

Robert suddenly felt a sharp pain in his back. Someone had thrown a suitcase at him. He turned around and saw a tall boy with curly hair pick up the case.

"Sorry mate, I thought you were one of the baggage handlers. Mine wandered off, and you guys are all interchangeable anyway."

The boy laughed with two friends.

Robert looked him directly in the eye. "You certainly look as if you couldn't carry your own bags." Robert extended his hand as the kid bristled. "I'm Robert. Where you gentlemen from?"

The boy didn't shake Robert's hand. He simply looked at him and spoke. "I'm Jacob, from Citadel province, in Temple City. This is Simon and Cole." Cole gave Robert a genuine smile and extended his hand despite Jacob's dirty look. Simon was waving at some girls and had forgotten any of them were there. Robert found the indifference more peaceful than Jacob's attention. Suddenly, Melissa bounced up to the group. Her bubbliness in person was precisely as Robert had expected.

She smiled at all of them. "Making friends, are we?"

Robert was about to reply when Jacob immediately said, "Oh, you know us," and hugged Melissa. He had noticed that Robert thought the question was for him, so he gave Robert a weird smirk. Melissa hugged Simon and Cole as well. Clearly, they all knew each other from Temple City.

“This is Robert. He was just about to tell us where he’s from.” That same smirk remained on Jacob’s face.

Robert extended his hand to Melissa. “Hi, I’m Robert.”

She smiled. “I saw you earlier.” He swallowed hard, as he’d just about had his limit of embarrassment, but she continued. “You might not have seen me, but I was walking with my mom...” She trailed off and gave Robert a warm smile. “How was your drive in?”

“Drive was good. A little long. I’m from Anton.”

“Exotic. Where’s that?”

“It’s one of the industrial provinces, just south of Trent.”

Jacob laughed. “She was only being polite. We’re all perfectly aware of that stinky province.”

“I think that’s great. Some of our greatest inventors came from Trent.” Jacob rolled his eyes at Melissa, but she kept going. “I like your shirt.”

Jacob moved between Melissa and Robert. “I think I had the same shirt four years ago and then gave it away. It's probably the exact same one,” Jacob started laughing.

With Melissa watching, Robert was suddenly no longer indifferent to someone trying to antagonize him. Anger filled his head. His father had always told him that if you’re already in a fight, you might as well win it. He had no idea if he was simply rationalizing what he was about to do or if his anger had complete control of him. He didn’t care. Robert stepped forward and punched Jacob in the nose. Jacob reeled back as his nose started to bleed. It was clear he hadn’t been in a fight before. A hundred parking lot scraps were in the back of Robert’s mind. He knew Jacob’s next move would be predictable. Jacob charged back at him and swung his right, overextending himself. Robert let Jacob’s momentum work against him as he dodged the blow and pulled him close, landing several jabs on his ribs. He then pushed Jacob down.

Jacob looked up at Robert from the ground. He wiped the blood from his nose.

“You had enough?” shouted Robert.

Jacob kept grinning. “You idiot.”

Suddenly, Robert felt two of Jacob's friends grab his arms. Jacob quickly jumped up and punched him in the face. Robert tried to squirm free but couldn't. Jacob hit him again. Robert was no longer caught by surprise, though. He slammed his foot down on top of one of the boy's feet, and the boy released him out of impulse. Robert bent over and launched his elbow into the boy's nose. He could feel it break. Now free, he turned and grabbed his other attacker's arm. He was filled with a rage he hadn't felt since childhood and was going to break it. Suddenly, he heard the shout: "Boys!"

Robert felt his muscles spasm and found himself on the ground. He saw Jacob on the ground as well. The pain subsided, but Robert wasn't yet able to stand. He looked around to see what had happened. He also saw Simon on the ground and another boy he hadn't met. It wasn't Cole who had been holding his arms. Cole stood back in a crowd that had formed. Robert took some comfort in the fact that Cole hadn't participated. There was a man in bright red standing above them. He held some gun he'd used on them. He spoke in a regal tone.

"Gentlemen, you're embarrassing your families. The Tests are a time to come together and prove yourselves. If you fail here, you'll certainly fail out there. All four of you boys need to come with me for disciplinary action. You'll have to wait until later to meet your pods."

The four boys lay there, still recovering.

"Get up and follow me right now!"

They slowly rose to their feet and started after the man. As Robert walked through the crowd, he brushed past Melissa and noticed her crying.

"Melissa! Did we accidentally hurt you? I'm so sorry."

"You boys are all the same!" She turned and hugged her girlfriends. Robert wanted to go to her, but the man called out again.

"Mr. Jacques, I think everyone has enjoyed your presence enough already. Come with me."

The four boys walked in silence down a series of hallways. Some were well-lit, and others dark, but all reminded Robert of a hospital. An arrow on the wall illuminated each of their names and pointed out the path they should take. It was as if the walls were one big terminal screen. The arrows grew lighter and eventually disappeared. They had stopped at nothing.

"Each of you will be in a separate room. Someone will be in to see you shortly."

Robert was about to ask where to go when the other boys pushed on small indents in the wall nearby. It was as if there was only an outline of a door, but when they pushed, a complete door appeared for them. Robert did the same with an indent near himself. He almost pressed too hard and stumbled into a small square room as it opened. The door closed behind him.

The white room only consisted of a table and two chairs. It reminded him of a police station he'd been in when he was younger. He sat down on the chair. His shirt was changing to a darker silver to try and hide the blood that was staining it. He had to admire its efforts; it was doing everything it could for them. He put his head on his arms and decided he would get some rest. He was ready to be sent home. His father was right.

Robert awoke suddenly. A man sat in the chair across from him. Robert didn't believe the man had said anything, Robert had simply woken up. He wondered how long the man had been sitting there. The man was older, with short gray hair and a wrinkled face that gave him a permanent warmth.

"Mr. Jacques, it's a pleasure to meet you. I'm Admiral Hill."

"Hi, sir. Apologies about taking a nap. It's a habit. I was always taught that as soon as you're ready to sleep, you should. You might not get that chance again."

Admiral Hill smiled. "That's a decision I respect, Mr. Jacques. I was in the army when I was younger. When I could eat, sleep, or go to the washroom, I always did. That chance might not come again, so you take it. I find any good theory can also be applied to beautiful women; this certainly holds. When you find one, you don't let the chance pass you by."

Robert smiled. "I agree with you, sir. Hard to believe that people told me I wouldn't learn anything useful during the Tests." The admiral chuckled slightly.

"Why are you here?"

"I got into a fight with that boy Jacob. I did some sneaky work on his ribs, so a medic or someone should ensure no serious damage."

"That little scrap of yours doesn't concern me at all. Reminds me of the Tests back in my day. Some of that energy is missing now. We've become complacent. Life should be a constant fight for something better, but we've lost that in recent years. I want to know why you came to the Tests."

"You aren't sending me home?"

"Not at all. I think it's fantastic you're here. It's been decades since we had any real level of participation from the perimeter provinces. Some would disagree, but I think we've stagnated as a society. Humans rise to conflict. We only get stronger by pushing against something. These past few years, people have entered the Tests knowing exactly where they'll end up, and they bring that same complacency to the life they lead when they leave these doors. Your being here is a step in the right direction. I need to know why you came."

Robert didn't know why he'd come. "I didn't want to come. I did it for my mother mostly. She wanted me to see what everything was like."

An anger flashed in Admiral Hill's face that hadn't been present before. "That answer is pathetic." The man stood up and headed toward the door.

Robert didn't know what to say but shouted, "More!"

The man turned around. "What's that?"

"More, sir. I wanted more and felt I could do more. That's why I'm here."

"That's excellent. Remember that when you're going through your Tests. Good luck."

With that, Admiral Hill pushed on the door and exited the room.

Robert was left alone in the room. He didn't want to make another scene, but it wasn't in him to wait. He stood up and pushed against the outline of the door on the wall. The hall was empty. There were no arrows this time, and he was walking through barren white hallways that all looked the same. He suddenly heard a cry of "help" up ahead. He rounded the corner into a large room. A small girl stood in the middle. She was crying and pointed a trembling finger at the room's far corner. That's when he saw it. In the far corner was a cage about five or six feet high. Inside was an animal that looked like it had the head of a hammerhead shark but with four legs and hooves. It was the size of a young horse but with none of the docility of those animals; it was rapidly throwing itself against the cage bars. Robert could see it would only be a few seconds before the bars gave out. He looked around the room. There was a sword in the far corner. He didn't know what that could do against a beast like this. There were three exits to the room. The corridor he had come in, a similar short corridor on the far side, and a large hallway down the left side. The top of the cage was a solid metal floor; he could try climbing up there and then to another ledge, but he couldn't see how he would get the girl up as well.

"Come with me, and don't say a word." Robert grabbed the girl and ran into the center of the room. There were two walls, standing alone, only about six feet long, with three feet between them. They were parallel and missing the required counterparts to make a room. "Stand right in the middle here. Don't make a sound, and don't move." The girl meekly nodded.

The beast broke through the bars and erupted from the cage. It leaped around the room erratically but slowed down at the walls. It circled the walls and then stopped and faced Robert. The walls were on either side. There was nothing between him and the beast. He could reach out and touch it. Robert put his arms around the girl and tried not to breathe. It stood there facing them, circled the walls once more, and then shot down the long hallway, rolling its head from side to side as it ran. Robert was shocked at the speed.

"You can speak now," Robert whispered.

"Why didn't it eat us?"

"Did you see its eyes? They were on the sides of its head. I figured it couldn't see anything directly in front of it. The walls on either side forced it to face us instead of looking at us from the side."

"Why didn't it run forward without knowing?"

Robert thought about it, a scary thought. "I guess I just thought it wouldn't. I mean, I could run backward right now, but if I was going to actually go in that direction I would always turn around first. I guess even beasts are uncertain about things sometimes."

The little girl wiped her face and extended the snot-covered hand to shake hands. Robert had to laugh at the gesture. "I'm Samantha. That was very brave and smart, what you just did."

He extended his hand and was about to grasp the girl's. "I'm Robert. You were very brave being quiet like that."

Robert heard a shrill voice behind him. "Mr. Robert Jacques! There you are." He turned around to see an older woman. She wore a blue uniform and a red headpiece. "What're you doing here, young man?"

Robert turned to look at the girl and realized he had closed his hand around nothing. She was gone. There was no trace of the beast or the cage. The room was empty. Robert wiped his eyes.

"I… I was lost."

"Well, follow me. I've been looking for you. You'll be late for the start of the Tests if you don't come quickly."

She started exiting the room, and he followed. The two of them walked through a convoluted maze of hallways. The arrows on the wall were clear and distinct, showing their names and where they were in the building. Robert looked over his shoulder, expecting the beast to barrel around a corner.

"What were you doing in that room? It's strictly off-limits."

"Every room here looks the same, so calling a particular one off-limits doesn't seem helpful." She didn't seem interested in Robert's jokes. "What's that room used for?"

"It hasn't been used in decades. It used to be used to identify and train soldiers. This is peacetime, though. No one has seen that room in a long time."

"Why do people carry guns if it's peacetime? I saw people with guns on their hips."

"Sometimes you don't know a threat until it's too late. Isn't that how you got in that fight today?" She drifted off. "You're lucky I'm only an administrator and not an evaluator, or I would mark you for wandering off. I might have given you some points for the fight, though." Robert could see the hint of a smile on her face.

They rounded the corner, and Robert saw rows of people sitting in an auditorium down a short hall. "Now, they're about to start the introduction. Please find a seat and stay out of trouble. This seating is your section."

"Thank you. What's your name?"

"I'm Ms. Raymore. Robert, good luck." With that, she hurried back down the hall.

The hallway opened into one of the largest auditoriums Robert had ever seen. Small drones hovered in the air, precisely projecting to each auditorium section what was happening on stage. The stage was in the middle but floated around to give everyone a view. Robert looked at his section of seating. The only seat was next to Cole. He felt sick. He was certain Jacob would show up wanting the seat, and it would start another fight. That was when he noticed Jacob sitting at the back. His arms were crossed. Cole must have chosen to sit alone. Robert walked to the seat and sat down.

Cole smiled. "Sorry about earlier, man. Those guys can be jerks. Honestly, though, I was ready to fight when it was fair."

Robert laughed. "Me too."

The boys fell silent as the lights in the auditorium dimmed. A man stepped on stage.

Cole leaned in. "That's the chancellor. Melissa's dad."

"Welcome to the Aptitude Tests. Our predecessors, before the Tests, used to spend decades deciding what to do with their lives and not start a profession until their twenties. That age was pushed even further for more complex professions our society truly valued. Worse than the time it took, individuals often spent significant time going down a particular path before they realized it wasn't for them. It wasted their resources, and it wasted the resources of our society. As jobs got more complex, and we needed to know more about each role, the problems only compounded. That all stopped with the Aptitude Tests!" The chancellor stepped back, and raucous applause filled the theater. Robert was caught off guard. He didn't know enough about it to understand which parts were good or bad. He continued to reserve his applause.

The chancellor continued. "I must warn some of you that the Aptitude Tests can be upsetting, depending on your hopes and dreams. It compounds a lifetime of disappointment into one day. I need all of you to understand that this is to prevent you from allocating your time and resources to endeavors you aren't suited for. The Tests save you time and energy. The best thing for society is having everyone do what they're best at. That's how we accomplish the most.

"Full transparency is important to ensure everyone buys into the system. I want to explain to all of you how this works. Everything you do over the next month is monitored. We all monitor it, and a supercomputer called Samantha watches everything. We are all the architects of the success and peace we've recently enjoyed. We take this responsibility very seriously." There was another round of applause.

Robert leaned into Cole. "I think I met Samantha."

Cole smiled. "Yeah, man, of course, she's everywhere." Cole raised his hands and waved them all around, mocking him. Robert had to laugh to himself at how it sounded.

The chancellor continued. "There are cameras in every room. She watches how you interact with others, do the tests, and handle every situation. It's all evaluated and computed. The result is an extrapolation of exactly how you'll perform in the real world. Samantha will flag this in advance if you don't have the temperament for certain jobs. Before this, people wasted their time, and, more dangerously, we had people in important positions that they should never have been in. Now, I want to introduce you to the senior evaluators." A group of twenty men and women stepped onto the stage. The chancellor introduced them; they'd all succeeded in their fields. The kids seated near Robert whispered about the evaluators as if they had met them. Some even sounded as if they were family friends and had vacationed together. Robert only knew the one that had paralyzed him earlier, which he assumed was worse than not knowing anyone.

Suddenly, he recognized one of them. "And here we have Mr. Demure." Robert was trying to remember where he recognized him from and realized it was his driver into Temple City. As Mr. Demure stepped forward, he seemed to look right at Robert and wink. Robert turned to see if anyone else had noticed; no one seemed to. Mr. Demure stepped back, and the chancellor continued to go through the other evaluators.

"Now, I wish you good luck! I look forward to speaking with all of you in a month, right here, and congratulating you on the lives that you'll live!"

The stage that the chancellor was on, floating in front of them only moments before, slowly lowered into the ground, and the floor closed over the top of it. The auditorium started to exit. Robert got into line behind Cole, not knowing where they were going. An administrator was leading the group of thirty kids sitting in his section. Robert could see Melissa walking with two girls up ahead. Eventually, they came to a large room with thirty beds in a row. The head of each bed backed against a wall with a closet in it. A desk with a complete terminal was set up next to each bed.

The administrator leading them stopped and turned. "My name is Dr. Alexander. I'll be the administrator for this group and direct you through the Aptitude Tests. What you see behind me are your quarters for the month. I know these conditions are tough, but you'll face many tough conditions in your life. How you deal with it will be evaluated." Robert had just been thinking that the quarters looked pretty good. He noticed a lone duffel on one of the beds and realized it was his. He'd completely forgotten that he'd left it during the commotion of the fight. "Please go to your bed and start unpacking. Your terminal has a calendar with a schedule for the month. Your first test is tomorrow. There's a full index of relevant materials loaded on your terminals. Study and prepare at your discretion. Like in life, you can make what you want out of the next month." Dr. Alexander finished his canned speech and left the room.

Robert went to his bed. He noticed the name on the bed beside him: "Melissa." He heard her sigh as she noticed it as well. She mumbled, "Hi again."

He smiled. "I guess it's pretty clear the beds were assigned, given you're next to me." Melissa smiled a little and kept unpacking.

Robert had hung up his few shirts in seconds. "Do you need help unpacking Melissa? I'm all done. Maybe I'm good at it, or I just didn't have much stuff."

"No thanks." She paused. "Not to be rude. It's just there's a lot of underwear and stuff." She giggled and blushed.

Robert laughed. "That would have slowed me right down, so it's probably for the best."

Robert put his hands behind his head and lay on the bed. Kids were logging into their terminals and reading through everything. He got up briefly and checked the calendar on his terminal. It said the first test was at nine a.m. All it said was "mathematical applications." There was a longer description, but Robert didn't care; he'd always been good at math. He closed his eyes and started to fall asleep.

He could hear people talking around him. Someone said, "Don't wake him. It's his fault." He opened his eyes to find Melissa shaking him. "We have a test in ten minutes," she whispered. Robert thought he was dead and that she was an angel. Instead of conveying this beautiful language, he only said, "What the hell?" He looked at his watch: *5:50 a.m.*

"Didn't you read the description on the terminal?"

Robert jumped to his terminal and opened the exam description: *The biggest part of any problem is reading and understanding it. This test will start three* hours before the scheduled time.

"Come on, we have to go right now." Melissa waved for Robert to follow her. The last of the kids were already leaving the room. "There's no time to get ready. Come with me." Melissa had to smile as she looked at Robert's shirt. Robert realized he'd worn his half-bloody shirt two days in a row. Robert laughed when he thought of how appalled his poor mother would be.

He followed Melissa. "Why would they do a weird trick like that? Your dad is the chancellor, right? Tell me why he'd do something like that?"

"My father and I see eye to eye on almost nothing, but I can see why it makes sense. There are a lot of confusing things in life. You can understand everything on your own, or you can be supported by people who help you. Either one of those things would get people to the exam this morning. I guess you passed because I wanted to wake you up." She smiled at him.

"Thank you."

They had arrived at a massive, all-white room. Thirty brown rectangular logs stood upright on the left side of the room.

The administrator stood in front of them. "Please line up on the far side of the room. Each of you needs to take a position in front of one of the logs." Robert picked a log beside Melissa. The administrator then handed out a red pole to each of them. It looked like a narrow telescope. As they stood there, the room started to rumble, and the floor before them collapsed completely. A chasm now stretched between them and the other side of the room. Robert thought it had all collapsed but noticed the floor had remained in certain places; everyone had three platforms in between them and the other side of the room. The kids all walked up to the edge and leaned over. Water was swirling around through the gaps almost twenty feet below them. Robert guessed that the raised parts were almost precisely four feet long on all sides. He'd been hunting many times with his father, and his depth perception was exceptional. The administrator turned and faced them.

"This is simple. That device you're holding will extend to any length you request; tell it what length. A small laser on the end can be used for cutting. The laser will only turn on if the end of the device is more than five feet away from the base of your log, forcing you to do some math. Measure your piece of wood, cut it into four pieces, and lay them across the gaps to get to the other side. Your piece of wood is a little more than thirty-two feet. I'm sure you all understand where this is going. The gaps are seven feet, eight inches." Kids were murmuring. "The pieces you're laying across weigh no more than a couple of pounds, so there's no disadvantage for not being as strong. We want to see your ability to solve problems under pressure. Once you've crossed using a piece of wood, that piece is locked to the floor. I must also stress that there's a time limit."

With that, the administrator pushed on the wall and exited the room.

Robert instantly knew what to do. The log he was cutting was at a right angle to the floor. He just had to know the two other sides of a triangle to understand what length he wanted. He thought about the number they'd given him. Eight feet. He knew they wouldn't make it too hard.

"Six feet." Robert's pole extended six feet. He turned the laser on to put an indent in the floor. He grabbed the pole and ran up to place the bottom where the indent was. "Ten feet." The pole extended ten feet. He slowly lowered the pole until it touched the piece of wood and turned the laser on. The bottom of the log separated and fell to the floor. He picked up the piece and set it aside. The administrator was right; it couldn't have weighed more than a couple of pounds, but it was solid. He stood the rest of the log back up and started the process again. Robert looked to see if he was behind the other kids. He was shocked to see that he appeared to be ahead of everyone. Some of the other kids were trying to cut their logs near the top, which made the math harder, while others seemed to understand exactly what to do, but they were moving at an excessively careful pace, and they'd fallen behind.

Robert finished cutting his four parts and laid the first across the gap. There were only two inches on either side, but it felt stable. Robert was able to hold all three remaining pieces in his arms as he stepped across. He put the second piece down and stepped across with the remaining two. He was smiling as he realized he was going to be first.

That's when he heard it: a slight sound that built to a roar. He looked back to see water pouring from the far wall. He was stunned to see what had become a roaring waterfall inside the room. The kids still cutting their pieces were losing their footing and getting washed off the edge. A kid he didn't recognize was banging on the door the administrator had exited through, but to no avail. The water kept increasing in force, and it started to move out from the wall, coming down from the ceiling. It was the wall now, and it was moving toward him. He watched as it hit kids still on the first podium; they instantly crumpled and were swept off the edge. A panic had set in as everyone was aware that the wall of water was advancing. Robert moved quickly and laid down his second to last piece, and stepped across. He looked back to see where the water was, and that's when he noticed Melissa. She was beside him on her last platform, but she'd cut the last one too short. Melissa stood on her platform with nowhere to go, watching the wall of water advance.

Robert called out to her. "Melissa! Get ready to catch."

"Don't! You need it!"

"I'll be fine. Walk in the park." Robert tossed his plank, and Melissa caught it. Her expression was torn, but now that she had it, she laid it down and stepped across.

Robert looked back. The wall of water was approaching the second platform. He tried pulling up the log that he'd previously laid down. He pulled as hard as he could, but they were stuck in place; the administrator was right. Melissa stood on the other side of the gap. He didn't have the heart to tell her that his only idea had been to force the previous piece of wood. He looked at the gap. Almost eight feet. He knew that was achievable, but the surface was slippery, and he was shorter than most. He took one step back and then launched himself. He wasn't going to make it. He hit the far side with his chest, and it knocked the wind out of him. He had his arms flat out on the edge. Part of him wanted to let go and fall. Melissa's arms were suddenly holding his hands and pulling. The two of them pulled him over the edge, and he rolled his legs over as the wall of water hit the edge and then disappeared. He looked around, meeting eyes with other shocked students who had made it across. No one was speaking as everyone caught their breath.

Melissa leaned toward him. "What you just did was so stupid."

"What? You saw how easy that jump was for me," Robert wheezed.

A door opened on the wall, and Dr. Alexander stepped out. "Well done everyone who made it. You'll get points in order of your completion time. We'll have a break for breakfast and then general cognitive ability tests all afternoon. I also wanted to let you know that all your classmates are fine. Some require medical attention, but most will be joining you at breakfast."

"I'm glad you're okay. Thank you!" Melissa hugged him, and he barely noticed the pain. "I'm going to stop by the infirmary to ensure my friend Jenny's okay." Melissa stepped back and waved goodbye.

Robert got to his feet and headed to the cafeteria. He was starving and loaded up his tray. There wasn't anyone he recognized, so he sat at a long silver table by himself.

It wasn't long before Melissa slammed her tray in front of him.

"That was a big risk you took for me."

"The way I see it, I wouldn't have been there if it wasn't for you. I'd have still been sound asleep in my nice, warm bed. That sounds much better now that I think about it."

"You could have drowned focusing on other people, or worse, finished last. This is for your career. They decide the rest of your life here, where you live, who you can be with."

"I'm sure it all shakes out as it should."

"You don't know much about the Tests, do you?"

"Nope." He took a bite of his apple. "I seem to be doing fine, though. That was a fun little challenge."

"No, that was different. I've never heard of anything like that in the Tests. Not in decades, at least. My brother went five years ago, and it consisted almost entirely of him writing exams at terminals. He became a doctor. Today, it was more like what they used to do during wartime. Gabriel, in our section, broke his arm when the water knocked him down. I'm surprised no one died. That's not how this is supposed to go. Didn't you see our administrator's face at the end? He was white as a sheet and looked shocked."

"Probably wondering why your father is such a dick to all those kids. Doesn't he organize all of this? Can't you just ask him why?"

"Don't say that! We don't talk." Her face flushed, but Robert didn't notice how upset she was; he thought she looked beautiful. She looked at him sternly. "You shouldn't sit alone. The cameras record everything, and the computer analyzes it. They'll assume you're less likely to make friends, less likely to be successful; it extrapolates your entire life from one month of actions."

"I'm not sitting alone."

"Yes, you are." Melissa picked up her tray and left.

Robert sighed and looked around. There was a small kid sitting alone. It wasn't the type of kid Robert would normally talk to, but neither of them seemed to have their pick of friends here. Robert moved his tray and sat down next to the kid.

"I'm Robert."

The kid looked ecstatic. "That was a pretty cool jump back there. Sorry, I'm Curtis."

Robert shook his hand. "So, you're in my section? That's great. You must have made it across if you're here eating."

"Yes. I was the first across. I think you'd have beat me though, if you hadn't stopped. I guess you were just showing everyone what other skills you have."

Robert laughed. "What do you think of all of this?"

"I think it's beautiful. It gets life down to a science. The evaluators and the computer watch everything we do. If you have enough input, you can predict anything in this world. That is what the Tests do. The computer's even scanning us right now. It checks our organs and everything. It can even extrapolate when we die."

"Why would when we die matter?"

"The government doesn't want to spend money training someone to be a physicist or doctor if they're going to die in a few years. It might as well send them to work in the plants in the industrial provinces." Curtis saw Robert's face. "Sorry. I didn't think there."

"It's okay."

"No, it's not. No one should talk like that. To be fair, I don't think anyone from the central provinces could have made that jump or even tried."

"Thanks, man. Do you know a lot of the kids here then?"

"I know some of them. I miss my family, though. My sister and I got into a big fight before I left. She's two years younger. I know I'll see her again in a couple of weeks, but I want to tell her I'm sorry." Curtis played with his food. "You spend your entire life preparing for this, and then you get here and realize that parts of your life before this might have been the most important."

A bell in the hall rang.

"That means it's time to move to our next activity. You can follow me if you like." Curtis was exceptionally polite.

A different administrator stood at the front of the hall and motioned for them to follow. The class slowly shuffled behind.

"Dr. Alexander is indisposed for now, so I'll be directing you now. Please follow me. We have a good old boring class scheduled for the afternoon." Robert thought he heard Curtis let out a little cheer.

They entered a classroom. Melissa and a couple of students with casts or bruises were already in some of the seats. It looked like the rest of their section had been released from the infirmary.

"Please sit down at a terminal. For five hours, you'll work through a series of questions on your terminal. Some examine your general cognitive ability, while others are knowledge-based. We'll return here for multiple sessions over the next few weeks. The wall at the front tracks your progress in every different category of question." A massive wall had their names and brightly colored columns for each question category. "Each question is worth one point. You can buy twenty-five more questions in a specific category but only by paying one point from every category. Each of you can sell your services for answering a specific number of questions in a category for points related to a different category. You sell the questions before answering them, so your track record on this board will be important to those buying them. It's a very fluid competition, and you should focus on your studying each night based on where you think the value is. You may begin."

Robert looked at his terminal screen. The other students were already clicking through questions. Even the kid with the cast appeared to be moving quickly. Terminals like this were rare and new to Robert. There was only one terminal like this at the plant, and no one had it in their homes. He pressed the screen and options for different questions came up. There was math, history, problem-solving, comprehension, physics, biology, chemistry, and psychology. Robert started doing some math questions but quickly got bored. The problem-solving was more interesting. He kept looking at Melissa, trying to get her attention. Robert clicked on the chat function on the terminal. He could see icons for everyone in the class. He clicked on Melissa and started typing.

Robert: I have questions for you.

Melissa: What questions would you complete? I'm short on biology.

Robert: I only have one question actually. Do you have a boyfriend?

Robert suddenly heard the class giggling. He looked up to the front of the room and saw his question on the screen; the text from all the chats in the class slowly scrolled along the right side of the screen.

The administrator smiled. "Mr. Jacques, before you say anything else, I must clarify that all chats are shown up here. It's so kids can understand the going rate for certain questions. That way, they might want to focus on a more valuable category and study for it in the evenings if it turns out that the rest of the class is bad at it. Each student has a chance to increase their own value as they would in society. By all means, though, don't let me stop you from spending this time the way you want."

Robert looked over at Melissa. Her face was flush, but she had a small smile.

Robert: Biology is fine.

The following day was the same, and so was the next. Robert played around on his terminal but wasn't as focused on completing questions as the other kids. During the evenings, the other students studied, but Robert often disappeared into the corridors of the building. He was looking for what he saw that first day—Samantha. After the fourth day in the classroom, Melissa pulled Robert aside back at their quarters.

"Why aren't you trying?"

She seemed angry, and Robert was surprised. "What do you mean?"

"You should be trying harder. That's the most important thing. They always say it's the greatest indicator of success. You're only answering a few questions during the day and don't even appear to be studying at night. I don't even know where you go. The computer will notice you aren't trying."

"Why does this make you so angry?"

"The Tests take everything into account, and then they tell you what you can and can't do in this world before you even know yourself. On the last day, you get a list of the career paths available to you and what provinces each of them could be in. Some kids get a hundred options. Other kids only get a few, or maybe only one. They're directing you to where you're most valuable; you have a choice, but you truly don't. Someone smart might think they should get every option and then be able to decide, but they would never let them go work in the mines. They would deem it a waste."

"What are you saying? Are you worried that I'll go back to the life I already have? Doesn't that sound insulting to look down at my life like that?"

"No. I'm worried you aren't giving us a chance to be together. If there's no overlap in our options, we can't go somewhere together."

A huge grin spread across Robert's face at the thought of this. "What if our only overlap is where we are both proctologists?"

Melissa smiled and pushed him. "Are you always this funny, or is it only for the cameras?"

"What do you mean?"

She scrunched her face in a way that somehow made it impossibly cuter.

"Everything's measured and weighed. Those cameras up there watch everything."

She pointed at little dark balls attached to the ceiling, each the size of a marble.

"What do you think the computer factors into the calculations? If I kiss you, does it see that as courage?"

She moved closer. "I think that'd be very beneficial to your ultimate score. Initiative is a big predictor of ultimate career success."

Their voices were whispers now. "Yes, I think this'll be the most beneficial thing I do here." He leaned in, and they kissed.

For the next week, Robert worked hard at the terminal during the day and studied at night. He'd noticed that the class was short on psychology knowledge. At the start, Curtis had been trading psychology answers to the other students, but they'd grown increasingly expensive as he realized no one else could provide them. Robert had started being able to trade answers more cheaply; he didn't get as many correct, but he was doing well and starting to catch up to the other students in points.

The next week, the administrator led the class past their usual classroom. He didn't say anything. The schedule for the day had said "testing." They rounded four more corners until the hallway opened into an impossibly large internal room. It was filled with what looked like a forest. Robert realized it wasn't the start of a forest but an actual wall of trees and bushes.

The administrator turned. "Welcome to your exam for the day. It should be a fun one." Robert's eyes were wide.

A kid behind the group called, "Is it just a big maze?"

The administrator gave them a scathing look. "It's much more technical than that, but yes, it's a maze. The course we've outlined presents you with a series of decisions. As with anything in life, you can decide where your time and resources will best be used."

The entire class stood in front of the maze. A large screen above the entrance showed all the walls and routes. Robert looked at it. Every route or obstacle was color-coded. Some were puzzles, others were physical challenges. At the end of the other side was a red dot.

The administrator kept talking. "As you can see, the destination is on the far side of the maze. You may begin."

Robert heard kids murmuring about older friends who had told them which routes were best. Everyone ran up to the map and studied it briefly. Kids were already starting to head into the maze at full speed. Curtis stared intently at the map, presumably studying all the walls and dead ends. Robert wondered if he was trying to memorize it all. Robert assessed everything and then suddenly started running as fast as he could to the right, outside the entrance to the maze. Robert was going around. He looked back to see if anyone had decided to follow him. No one had. His pace had likely discouraged them.

Robert had been running for half an hour, tracking right along the side of the maze, when he saw her standing there. To his left was the exterior of the maze, and to his right was the room's wall. Directly in his path was the girl. Samantha.

She spoke first. "What are you doing out here?"

"I have to get to the other edge of the maze. A lot of the kids knew tricks on where to go and what to do. Without knowing anything about the maze, I figured my best bet was to go all the way around. I'm fast, and the other kids already knew so much about it; the one thing they might not have thought about is to go around."

"That's an interesting approach." Samantha looked at him. She was expressionless; there didn't seem to be a lot of child in her.

The two of them simply stared. Finally, Robert spoke. "Why haven't you challenged me again? Is it because of my performance in the classroom? I've been looking for you. I've been looking for that room where we first met."

The girl gave a little smile. "You don't need to look for challenges. There are things in this world, right in front of you, that need challenging. Those are the toughest ones." With that, the little girl disappeared.

Robert kept running around the maze. When he arrived, the administrator said he placed fourth. All he could think about was what the girl had said.

Over the next few days, Robert and Melissa studied together every night. Each day was a series of challenges or more time in the classroom. Robert had gotten to the point where he was ranked a competitive tenth in the class. Curtis liked him and had also been willing to help him study.

At the start of the last week, the administrator stepped into the room in the morning. "One more week. We'll start it off with a fun test." The schedule said it would be a full-day test of their understanding of the sciences.

The students followed the administrator to a room full of tables, but they weren't like anything Robert had seen. Each table had a glass top with thick walls. Part of the glass top had an electronic screen, and part looked like it would pull back; below that part, the desk was empty, as if it were a container. The sides of the desk ran to the floor. Each desk was in a pair of two. Robert was walking in with Curtis, and the two grabbed desks beside each other.

An administrator they hadn't seen before was standing in the classroom. He was already starting a speech. "The reason we test diagnostics is because, in many respects, it exemplifies life. You're faced with limited information, yet the world demands a decision. When the contest starts, a small pig will appear in your cube. The computer will instantly show the pig's temperature, an X-ray on the screen, and a summary of symptoms. On your terminal on the left, you can scroll through a hundred tests and a couple hundred thousand antibiotics, antidotes, etc. The pig's responsiveness to any treatment option has been accelerated for this exam. All the tests are described. You need no prior medical knowledge. The test will last for five hours. Whoever saves the most lives wins. What we're giving you is the biological equivalent of an animal, but it's not an actual animal, so there's no reason to let empathy slow you down. It never should. Proceed."

Robert was doing surprisingly well three hours later despite his lack of knowledge. He had realized that the score at the front of the room depended on the number of pigs you cured. If Robert didn't save the pig with his first guess, then he knew he probably never would. He'd quickly give it a lethal dose of an antidote or medicine, way more than it needed. The dosage would kill the pig, the machine would quickly dispose of it, and the back of the desk would open and put a new pig in front of him.

Robert suddenly heard Curtis's scream. He looked over and saw the pig in front of Curtis moving violently. Robert realized it wasn't only the pig; its skin was moving. Something was aggressively eating the pig's flesh. Curtis had taken his glove off and was holding up his hand, screaming; the same thing was happening to his hand and moving up his arm.

An alarm started going off in the lab, and the word "quarantine" was repeated on a loudspeaker. And if Curtis's scream hadn't gotten people's attention, a red light had also started flashing. An evaluator ran into the room and asked everyone except Curtis to exit immediately through a glass sliding door in the back. The class ran for the door. Robert remained next to Curtis. Curtis kept shouting for help but was frozen in place as he screamed and looked at his hand. Everyone but Robert and Curtis had now exited the lab. The evaluator screamed at Robert, "I'm locking down this lab. If you don't leave right now, you'll be trapped in here until we know the situation is contained."

Robert said one word: "No." The evaluator shook his head and slammed his hand on a red button near the door; the door slammed shut. The class was on one side, Robert and Curtis on the other. Robert looked around the room for anything to help Curtis. There was a side room at the back. Robert went through it, looking for an aid kit or anything, but it was barren. He shouted at Curtis.

"Curtis, can I order anything on the desk to cure this?"

"No! I looked, and they don't have the correct cure. I was about to ask the administrator why they gave me one that couldn't be solved when I noticed it had jumped to my arm. You should have left me!"

Robert suddenly motioned for Curtis to follow him to the side room. Curtis quickly followed. Whatever it was, it was almost halfway up his arm already. The class watched through the far glass door.

“Was there something in here to help?” Curtis looked hopeful between bouts of pain.

“There was nothing… I need you to hold your arm out here.” Robert told Curtis he needed to extend his arm into the side room.

Robert hovered his hand over the same red button the evaluator pressed to close the other door. He looked at Curtis. “You ready?” Curtis suddenly realized what Robert was planning. He nodded and clenched his teeth.

Robert pressed the button. Another emergency door slid across. It cut Curtis’s arm clean off as it closed; the arm fell to the ground in the other room. Curtis screamed and started shaking. His arm had to be cut near the shoulder, and it was gushing blood. Robert ripped off his shirt to tie it, but it was difficult, given the size of the wound.

“Curtis, what should I do now?” Curtis was going in and out of consciousness and didn’t respond.

Robert shouted at the evaluator and the class just outside the far glass door. “Come inside and help. It’s fine now. Look! You’re letting him die!”

No one replied. The evaluator held up his hand, signaling the class to hold back.

Robert kept screaming at them, but they stared. He could feel Curtis fading, and then he was gone. He lay there with him for five minutes until a group of people entered the room in head-to-toe white gear. They were spraying some foam everywhere and then exited a few minutes later. Robert was too shocked to move.

The glass door opened, and the class slowly shuffled back into the lab. The evaluator calmly asked them to wait quietly, but the exact opposite happened: kids cried, some were sick, and others shouted that the evaluator had refused to let them help. Robert was still in shock as a team in suits picked up the body of Curtis and left the room. He stood there covered in blood, not talking to anyone.

Jacob walked up to Robert. “That was very brave, man. Very brave.” Robert didn’t notice the compliment, and Jacob returned to the group.

Finally, there was a commotion at the back of the room, and the chancellor entered. He stepped to the front to speak.

"I want to commend all of you on your performance today. All of you did the right thing by leaving the room. Sometimes, there's nothing that can be done to save someone. You proved yourselves by following the orders of the evaluator during the lockdown. Almost all of you." The chancellor looked at Robert.

Robert broke out of his shock and shouted, "You did this to him! Your team forgot to put a cure in the terminal. He didn't have a chance."

The chancellor stared at them. "That was deliberate. It was important to see how you reacted, and it'll be important to see how the loss affects you going forward. Curtis had a heart that was impaired. It was picked up on the scans. He might as well have had a bomb inside him. It could have been days or six months at most. This was a worthy use of his life. Sometimes, we must do this to see how you will respond. Loss is an important challenge of life."

"He had a sister he didn't say goodbye to! You can't do that!"

"If you'd gotten some of the bacteria on you while trying to save him, you wouldn't be here arguing with me. Maybe next time you will... get some on you. Oh, and congratulations on getting the top score, Robert. You're a shining example." The chancellor pointed at the screen at the front of the class; Robert was first.

"How can we continue to participate in this? Everyone involved in the Tests should be ashamed. What if we quit?"

The chancellor smiled. "I don't believe your classmates would be joining you." Robert noticed that the class was dead quiet in the chancellor's presence. "If you want to quit, go ahead. The Tests sometimes do that to individuals. All it means is that you would have also quit in real life. There's plenty of hardship in the world. Don't be surprised that you also find it here."

Melissa was fuming and stepped up to stand beside Robert. She spoke slowly and deliberately. "I don't want to see you again, here, and after this. You embarrass me, and I carry that shame."

The chancellor looked at everyone. "Good day. Good luck with the remainder of the Tests."

Over the next few days, Robert could barely focus. All he could think about was that the society he wanted desperately to be a part of could do something like that to a person. The days passed as if they were for others, not himself. As a reflection of this mood, his position in the rankings was starting to drop.

It was already the final day when he came out of his daze. Melissa and Robert sat beside each other in the auditorium, waiting for the results. The chancellor and the other evaluators appeared on the floating stage. The chancellor stepped to the front and spoke.

"Today is easy. Under your chairs is a thin screen. In a couple of seconds, we'll populate your screen with the available options. When you head home today, you'll have a month to decide which choice you want to proceed with. I congratulate all of you. Together, we'll build a stronger society. You may now read your choices!"

Robert reached under his chair and picked up the thin screen. Melissa already held hers.

"You read yours first, Melissa."

Melissa clicked the screen, and dozens of options appeared. A series of different provinces and professions. He knew without scrolling through them that Anton wouldn't be on there; it wasn't the best use of resources.

"Your turn, Robert."

Robert had never been more nervous. He pulled up his screen. Robert wanted something he hadn't even been able to articulate until a couple of weeks before. He wanted more.

He clicked his screen. Only one option appeared. *Plant Manager, Anton*.

Robert didn't have a single joke in him. He was silent. He couldn't hide his disappointment. After all his work, he'd believed a different life was possible.

Melissa finally broke the silence. Her voice was shaky, but she tried to be supportive. "That's a more senior job than your father's, right? That's great. He'll be very proud."

Robert couldn't speak. His mouth was dry. She looked at him with wet eyes, waiting for his reply. He started to open his mouth, but the chancellor's voice rang out again.

"Congratulations all of you! That concludes the Aptitude Tests."

The chancellor waved, and the stage he was on started to retreat to the floor. Melissa was trying to say goodbye, but her words flowed around Robert like waves, and he was a rock. He couldn't think of anything except the smug chancellor retreating into the floor. He thought of something his father had said, and something came over him. Robert stood on his seat and jumped to grab the drone that floated before them, projecting an image of the stage. He held tightly to the drone. It started dropping in the air, but he was counting on that as he directed it toward the disappearing stage. The stage had just gone beneath the center floor, and the sides of the floor were starting to close over the top of it. Robert was close now as the drone dropped in elevation. The floor was almost closed when he let go, dropped, and rolled into the tiny gap before it closed completely.

Robert found himself in a room below the stage. The ceiling had just closed above him. The chancellor and the other evaluators had been talking; they were so shocked by his presence that they didn't even move. They stared. Robert quickly grabbed the gun off the belt of the evaluator closest to him. He pointed it at the chancellor.

The other evaluators realized what had happened, and they reached for their guns. Robert shouted at them, "No one move! I'll shoot the chancellor."

The evaluators froze. The chancellor held up his hands and spoke. "That isn't a stun gun, like what we used on you at the start. That's a real gun you've grabbed there. Why? What do you want, Robert?"

Robert was so angry that he was stammering. "You stole from me... You stole my future."

"This often happens when people aren't satisfied with their options. I mean, never to this extent, but we understand your frustration. You didn't have the temperament for a lot of options. You're smart, but you're a danger. I mean, look where we stand right now. There are certain ways we need to behave, that all of us need to behave, that allow our society to move forward. I must take a global view in my role here."

"That's not fair! I only stand here right now because I must! This shouldn't be the case. Samantha was challenging me for something bigger. I saw her. She spoke to me."

"She doesn't speak to anyone, Robert. I'm sorry, but you aren't special."

"That's not true!" Robert fired a warning near the chancellor's head to show he was serious. The chancellor put his hands up.

"Okay. Okay. Maybe she did talk to you. To be honest, I'd have no idea. We don't entirely understand how she works. She's an AI. She projects what everyone can do in their life, and we use that to sculpt our society."

"Why did I only get one option? Tell me the truth! You've probably never had someone here with nothing to lose so I hope you truly understand what that means." Robert fired another warning shot.

"Okay, the truth." The chancellor looked at the gun and then calmed his breathing. He slowly licked his lips, and it was as if a small smile appeared as he started to speak again. "The Aptitude Tests don't evaluate your ability to succeed. They evaluate your risk to the establishment. We take those who aim to defy the status quo and hide them in menial jobs in provinces as far away from Temple City as possible. That way, they have fewer tools available to them. After a while, they all find mediocrity. Intelligent men, men like your father. That's how we've done it for a long time. No one truly wants inequality to end; people just want to be on the winning side of it. At first, we thought this would only be temporary. Get the right people into the right jobs earlier, and they'll figure out how to create enough for everyone. But humans aren't good at sharing. It's become easier in recent years, though. People can become so certain they don't deserve a certain type of life that they stop trying altogether. But I'll tell you this, Robert, you put that gun down, and you can live the life you want. You can come to Temple City. The computer calculated that there's a ninety percent chance you marry Melissa if circumstances allow you to continue seeing each other."

"How can you let me do that?"

"Because, frankly, how could you ever tell anyone? You'd be just as much a part of the system as we'd be. Do you want the world to know you bought into a system that enslaves the people you grew up with? You won't be telling anyone. Now put that gun down."

Robert thought about it. "I can't let you continue your work."

The chancellor started to reach for his gun, and Robert shot him in the shoulder. For a second, they were both shocked.

"You idiot!" The chancellor screamed. He dropped to his knees and held his shoulder. "Shoot him!"

Robert braced himself as some of the evaluators raised their guns. A blast erupted, but it wasn't what he expected. Shocks had come from the walls, paralyzing some of the evaluators. Others, such as his driver, Mr. Demure, remained unharmed. Samantha appeared in the room. She wore her tiny smile.

"Hello, Robert. This was your final test."

Robert kept his gun raised and rubbed his eyes with his other hand. "What? Test for what?"

"These are war times. The chancellor has been running a totalitarian regime. I needed to know that you and those by his side were strong enough to stand up to it. I've calculated that several individuals, such as Mr. Demure here, will back you in your push for change."

"Why would you go to all this trouble if it was just to get rid of him?"

"Sometimes you need to go down a dark path to see who enjoys it and, more importantly, who is willing to stop it."

"But what happens now?"

"All of this is yours, Robert. All of this. You're in charge now. That's the option you've received here today."

www.ingramcontent.com/pod-product-compliance
Lightning Source LLC
LaVergne TN
LVHW091052150826
845673LV00002B/559

* 9 7 8 0 9 9 5 8 1 7 3 0 2 *